修編序

「**求職英語**」自出版以來，廣受讀者歡迎，為因應日新月異的求職市場，我們重新修訂，提供讀者最新資訊。

本書於修訂後，共分為四大篇章，從給求職者的建議、如何撰寫求職信函，到準備面試應答，蒐集就業資訊，各種資料樣樣俱全，編者深信，「**求職英語**」必定能夠幫助讀者，輕易地在競爭激烈的職場中，脫穎而出。

首先，第一篇「**自傳·信函篇**」教您，如何撰寫出色的求職信函。一封文情並茂、資訊齊備的自傳或履歷，是幫助您開啓面試之門的鑰匙，為了使您和其他的應徵者區別開，建議您不妨同時準備一份中文及英文應徵函，除了可以充分表達您的才幹，還能加深雇主對您的專業印象。本書以英漢對照的方式，仿照正式應徵函格式，給讀者最佳典範，讓您以最完善的準備，捷足先登。

第二篇「**面試必問考題**」的內容，包含在各方面可能被問及的考題，這絕對是使您獲得雇主青睞的秘密武器。無論是碰到一對一的面談，還是集體式的面談，只要詳讀本篇所提供的筆試準備重點、面試成功要訣、面試衣著秘訣，與萬變不離其宗的面試必問考題，您必定能以最佳狀態，輕鬆自如地在面試過程中，得到面試官的青睞，進一步搶得人人稱羨的金飯碗。

第三篇「**面試實況會話**」，搜羅了八大熱門行業的面試實況會話，不僅列出最常出現的面試問題，還提供了不同的答題方向供讀者參考。讀者可依自己的專長和才能，於參閱第四篇的「建議使用字彙」後，組合出適合描述自己的文句。一個不落俗套，且又能充分表達自我的回答，將是使雇主對您印象深刻的不二法門。

最後一篇「**補充資料**」，精心蒐集了所有最新求職資訊。面對目前一職難求，人人搶破頭的求職市場，光是會寫履歷，懂得充分表達自己還是不夠的，想要在接近飽和的求職市場中謀得一職，必須要知道，這是個「人求事」的時代，如何找到求職的途徑，才是最重要的。

有鑑於此，本書集結了公私立就業輔導機構、網站的資料，及「考選部年度考試計劃表」，和「陸軍志願軍官徵選辦法」。此外，爲了能找到比鐵飯碗值錢的金飯碗，本書還介紹了「六大必考證照」與「最佳在職進修管道」，有助於求職者以最佳姿態進駐職場。最後，本書還附有「羅馬拼音對照表」與各類資訊英譯表，供讀者參考。

本書的修編工作，係經多方蒐集最新資料，及審愼的斟酌與校閱後才完成。但仍恐有不足或錯漏之處，誠盼各界先進不吝指正。

王淑平　謹識

目　錄

3. 面試實況會話

4. 補充資料

A Suggestion to the Job Hunter
給求職者的建議

給社會新鮮人

根據統計資料顯示，台灣每年約有 15 萬個剛從大專院校畢業，準備投入就業市場的社會新鮮人。但近幾年經濟成長緩慢，企業開放給新鮮人的員額迅速萎縮，如何跨越求職門檻，找到一份與所學相關，且薪資足以糊口的工作，已成爲社會新鮮人的最大考驗。其實，只要就業前做好充分的準備，必定能找到適當的工作，遠離「畢業即失業」的惡夢。

就業前最重要的課題，便是**心理的調適**。在學校裏，年輕人是受到保護的一群，出了社會就得除去凡事依賴的心理，獨自面對複雜的人、事。所以，就業前，必須培養獨立自主的能力，碰到困難時，要能自己想辦法解決。社會的複雜與多元化，固然使年輕人必須面對重重難關，但從另一方面來說，挑戰性愈高，就能獲得愈多的成長與歷練。

第二重要的課題，是關於**職業的選擇**。選擇職業應該考慮下列幾項：自己的性向、興趣、能力、學歷，以及社會環境的需要。社會新鮮人要有從基層做起的決心，不要好高騖遠，要把眼光放遠。待遇高的工作，假如不具發展性，就不能算是好的工作。複雜的環境與繁重的工作量，也許正提供了自我磨練的機會。

再來是**知識與技能的充實**。在決定求職的方向之後，要立即充實與該行業相關的技能。例如：想當秘書的人，應該學會如何使用電腦；對雜誌編輯有興趣的人，應該充實大衆傳播方面的知識。即使唸的是應用性較高的科系，如工程、圖資、電機，也必須注意理論與實際的差距與配合，以做好充分而完善的準備。

此外，剛踏出校園的社會新鮮人必須明白，每年準備求職者爲數龐大，事求人，人求事，很難在短時間內找到稱心如意的工作。所以，不要因爲一時找不到適當的工作就氣餒了，要再接再勵，永不放棄。

給計畫換工作者

或許你才畢業一、二年，也或許你已經工作了十年以上，在決定換工作之前，不妨試著問問自己：「我爲什麼要離職？」如果對這個問題不加以探討，很可能會一輩子都在換工作。

通常辭職的動機不外乎下列幾項：

1. **打算進修、深造**——例如想繼續唸研究所、EMBA，或出國進修。這些原因多半不是突發的，可能在就業之前就已經計畫好了，也可能是在工作期間逐漸形成的。屬於這種動機的人，只要評估進修課程是否合乎所求，當前的經濟能力是否足以負擔，以及未來學以致用的可能性等，即可迅速決定。

2. **工作缺乏發展及升遷的機會**——這是「跳槽」的主因。處於這種情況的人必須注意，新工作一定要能讓自己有一展長才的機會，否則會導致一再換工作，連續的挫折很容易磨損一個人的鬥志。很多自認爲懷才不遇而終日鬱悶的人，就是這樣形成的。

3. **對工作性質、工作環境、或公司制度不滿**——因爲這種情況而離職的人最多，所以我們最好先了解一個事實：以目前的經濟狀況與就業市場而言，要找到一個性質、環境、制度皆合己意的工作，是可遇而不可求的。甚至可以說，只要這三項條件中，有一、二項合意，就十分難得了。切記！下一個工作不見得會更好！

針對計劃換工作者的情況，在此提出兩個建議：①**抽空參加進修、研習課程，充實專業知識與技能**。唯有本身所具備的條件提升，才有機會選擇更好的工作。②**克服心理障礙，調整心態**。有些人會埋怨工作的種種，是因爲跟別人作比較。見到認識的朋友、同學有所成就，或有滿意的工作，就不平衡。其實我們應該要了解，每個人的才能有高低之分，機運有好壞之別。當然，如果自認爲有能力找到更理想的工作，就不妨朝第①項所談的方向努力，則必能有所成就。如果自知才能平平，只要安分守己，盡忠職守，同樣能享受工作的樂趣。

最後，還有一個重要的建議，提供給社會新鮮人及計劃換工作者：**儘快確認自己的性向**（可以在學校，或就業、心理輔導機構，參加性向測驗，或向心理專家諮詢）。因爲有很多在工作中受挫的人，是由於本身的性向問題。所以與其成天埋怨，不如早點確認究竟是性向有問題，還是工作有問題。如果是個性須作調整，就得力求改變，否則再怎麼換，也找不到好工作。相反地，如果是工作崗位確實不宜久留，也應該及早作打算，以免錯失發展的良機！

本書製作過程

本書之所以完成，是一個團隊的力量。非常感謝美籍老師 Laura E. Stewart 和謝靜芳老師細心的校訂，白雪嬌小姐負責設計封面及美編，也要感謝黃淑貞小姐負責版面設計，以及戴叡華小姐協助整理資料。

1. Autobiography & Letter

自傳・信函篇

1 求職自傳、信函寫作要領
The Essentials of Writing Autobiography & Letter

應徵時所寫的自傳或信函，其目的在於獲得面談，或增加錄取的機會。因此，**撰寫時務必賦予特色**，避免平舖直敘，才能吸引對方。然而所謂特色，並不是誇大不實或標新立異，而是要將自己的專長及應徵理由適當地表達出來，讓對方覺得眞正需要你。所以內容的撰寫，應遵守兩大原則：「**誠懇**」與「**信心**」。

一份完整的自傳，通常包括下列各點：

1. **個人基本資料**：如姓名、性別、年齡、住址、電話、家庭狀況、專長、個性等。
2. **學歷**：教育過程、學校名稱、主修及輔修科目等。
3. **工作經驗**：如公司名稱、所任職務、工作性質、工作成就等。
4. **理想與抱負**：如離開原公司的原因、前來應徵的理由、對這份工作的展望等。

但若上述資料在履歷表中已填寫詳盡，則可選擇一些重點來加深印象即可。至於應徵函、自傳函、推薦函等的撰寫，則須依其目的，把握重點。因此內容與自傳、履歷重複者，可斟酌刪減。甚至也可將自傳與應徵函或自薦函合併，不必拘泥於形式。

自傳、信函的敘述方式，應把握「**簡明扼要**」的原則，絕不可咬文嚼字，賣弄文筆。而且字體要工整，不可潦草，更不能寫錯別字。

最後，還有一點須注意：不同的公司或職務，所要求的條件必不相同，因此，應徵一個以上的工作時，須弄清楚，使用同樣的自傳信函是否恰當。如不妥當，則應加以修改增減，甚至重新撰寫，方爲上策。

2 英文書信格式簡介
Application Letter Style

信封寫法

1. 郵票應貼在（信封）正面右上角。
2. 寄信人姓名、地址寫在正面左上角。
3. 收信人姓名、地址寫在正面的中央或右下四分之一處（見附圖）。

Dick Wilson
206 Queen's Road West ⬅ 寄信人
Hong Kong

Mr. Jack Liu
No. 11, 4F, Lane 200
收信人 ➡ Tung Hwa Street
Taipei, Taiwan
R.O.C.

也有人將寄信人姓名、地址寫在信封背後，收信人姓名地址寫在信封正面的中央。

Mr. Jack Liu
No. 11, 4F, Lane 200
Tung Hwa Street
Taipei, Taiwan
R.O.C.

✉ 信文寫法

No. 11, 4F, Lane 200
Tung Hwa Street
Taipei, Taiwan
R.O.C.
January 2, 2003

1. 寄信人地址 (The Heading) ➡

Mr. Michael Johnson
116 Seventh Avenue
New York, N.Y. 11216
U.S.A.

⬅ 2. 收信人姓名地址 (Inside Address)

⬇ 3. 稱呼 (The Salutation)

Dear Mr. Johnson,

⬇ 4. 信文 (內容) (The Body)

5. 結尾謙稱 (The Complimentary Close) ➡

Yours sincerely,

George Lee

6. 簽名 (The Signature) ➡ George Lee

P.S.

⬆ 7. 補述 (The Postscript)

標準英文地址寫法

66 Sinyi Rd., **Sec. 1**, Taipei	台北市信義路**一段 66 號**
6th Fl., 66, Anhe Rd., Sec. 1, Taipei 【根據郵政總局公佈的地址寫法，「安和」應寫成 Anhe 而不是 *Anho*。】	台北市安和路一段66號**6樓**
6th Fl., 66, **Lane 6**, Jhonghua Rd., Sec. 1, Taipei	台北市中華路一段 **6 巷** 66 號 6 樓
Rm. 609, 6th Fl., 66, **Alley 16** Lane 6, Ren-ai Rd., Sec. 1, Taipei	台北市仁愛路一段 6 巷 **16 弄** 66 號 6 樓 **609 室**
66 Sinyi Rd., **Sec. 2**, Taipei	台北市信義路**二段** 66 號
66 Ren-ai Rd., **Sec. 3**, Taipei	台北市仁愛路**三段** 66 號
106 Jhongsiao **E. Rd.**, Sec. 1 Taipei	台北市忠孝**東路**一段106 號
106 Nanjing **W. Rd.**, Taipei	台北市南京**西路** 106 號
66 Dunhua **N. Rd.**, Taipei	台北市敦化**北路** 66 號
66 Fusing **S. Rd.**, Taipei	台北市復興**南路** 66 號
4th Fl., 11, Lane 200, Tonghua **St.**, Taipei	台北市通化**街** 200 巷 11 號 4 樓
52 Jhongjheng Rd., Tamshui **Township**, Taipei **County**	台北**縣**淡水**鎮**中正路 52 號
19 Jhonghua Rd., Taishan **Town**, Taipei County	台北縣泰山**鄉**中華路 19 號
36 Jhonghua Rd., Kuanyin **Village** Kuanyin Town, Taoyuan County	桃園縣觀音鄉觀音**村**中華路 36 號

※路名有三種寫法，如：Sinyi, Sin-yi 或 Sin Yi，以第一種較常用。

3 Example of Autobiography 1

I was born and raised in Keelung, Taiwan, the northern port city near Taipei. I am the second son in my family and was born on April 7, 1979. Our family is financially stable, thanks to my father's diligent and consistent work — he is now an executive director of a leading Keelung bank. I plan to follow in his successful footsteps.

All of my family are Christian and have regularly attended church since before I can remember. I in particular have been involved in numerous church organizations and activities, and I have served as the president of our church's youth group. In addition, I was a boy scout until I entered Taiwan University in 1998.

I studied hard throughout high school, earned good grades, and scored well on the college entrance examination, so I was able to attend the prestigious Taiwan University. I am now a senior in its Business Administration Department, set to graduate in only a few months.

I hope that while you consider my application for this position you will bear in mind that I am an active, responsible and hard-working person, and as such would have only a positive effect on your company's business relations. Thank you for considering my application.

自傳範例 1

我生長於台灣省基隆市，鄰近台北的一個北方港市。一九七九年四月七日出生，在家中排行老二。由於父親勤勉又有固定的工作，我們家的經濟狀況非常穩定，父親現在是基隆市一家主要銀行的常務董事。我打算跟隨父親成功的腳步。

我們全家都是基督徒，而且從我有記憶以來，就定期上教堂。我還特別參加過很多教會的組織及活動，並且曾經擔任我們教會的青年團契會長。此外，我在一九九八年進入台灣大學就讀以前，一直都參加童子軍。

我高中時非常用功，獲得優良的成績，並在大學入學考試中得到高分，因此得以進入一流的台灣大學就讀。我現在是台灣大學企管系四年級學生，再幾個月即將畢業。

我衷心盼望您在考慮我對這個職位的應徵時，能夠記得，我是一個主動、負責，而且勤奮的人，這些特質對貴公司的業務關係將有正面的影響。謝謝您將我的應徵列入考慮。

**

executive〔ɪgˈzækjutɪv〕*adj.* 執行的；行政的
leading〔ˈlidɪŋ〕*adj.* 主要的；領導的
involved〔ɪnˈvɑlvd〕*adj.* 參與的
scout〔skaʊt〕*n.* 童子軍　　score〔skɔr〕*v.* 得分
prestigious〔prɛsˈtɪdʒɪəs〕*adj.* 聲望很高的；一流的

Example of Autobiography 2

I was born on August 14, 1967 in Taichung, Taiwan, Republic of China. My father is an airline pilot and my mother is a dentist. I have three sisters and a brother.

After graduating from the First Girls' Senior High School of Taipei in 1985, I attended National Cheng Kung University in Tainan, majoring in economics. I received my bachelor's degree in June, 1989, and have since worked at the government's Directorate General of Budget, Accounting and Statistics in several capacities. I have been promoted on the average of once every six months, but I fear that without a master's degree I cannot climb much higher. I've, therefore, decided to seek employment in the private sector.

I sincerely hope that you will give me the opportunity to explain more of my capabilities to you in a personal interview. I believe I would be of great value to your company. Thank you.

自傳範例 2

我是一九六七年八月十四日，在中華民國台灣省台中市出生。父親是航空公司的飛行員，母親是牙醫師，家中有三個姊妹及一個弟弟。

一九八五年，我從台北第一女子中學畢業後，進入台南國立成功大學就讀，主修經濟。一九八九年六月得到學士學位，然後就在主計處擔任數項職務，平均每半年晉升一次。但我擔心沒有碩士學位，我將無法升到更高的職位，因此決定在私人機構找一份工作。

我衷心期望您能給我機會，在面談時說明我的其他才能。我相信我對貴公司而言，是具有極大的價值。謝謝。

** ——————————————

Directorate General of Budget, Accounting and Statistics 主計處
capacity〔kəˈpæsətɪ〕*n.* 地位；職位
master's degree 碩士學位　　sector〔ˈsɛktɚ〕*n.* 部門
capability〔ˌkepəˈbɪlətɪ〕*n.* 能力；才能

Example of Autobiography 3

I was born in Shalu, Taiwan on September 3, 1976, and raised in a happy family that included my father, mother and younger sister. When I was still quite young our family moved to Kaohsiung, where I received all of my formal education up to and through my four years at National Sun Yat-sen University. I graduated in 1998 with a B.S. in Mechanical Engineering. I earned my master's in 2002 in the same field at the University of Washington in Seattle.

Even in my childhood I exhibited a fascination with machines. I often built my own inventions, without ready-made plans or parts, and even won a number of science fairs with some of them. Recognizing this as being more than just a casual interest, my parents encouraged me throughout high school to study mathematics and the sciences especially hard.

I have just recently returned to Taiwan from the United States and hope to find employment which will allow me to both serve my nation and put to use much of the knowledge I gained in my years of study. Though I haven't any work experience, I believe my academic record proves that I am a steady, diligent, imaginative and earnest worker.

自傳範例 3

我是一九七六年九月三日在台灣的沙鹿出生，家庭生活美滿，家中有父親、母親和妹妹。在我很小的時候，全家搬到高雄，並在當地接受正規教育，直到在國立中山大學四年畢業。我於一九九八年畢業，取得機械工程的學士學位，並在二〇〇二年於西雅圖華盛頓大學，取得相同領域的碩士學位。

我從小就很喜歡機器，常常自己發明東西，而不用現成的設計或零件，甚至還以其中一些創作，在科學展覽中獲得不少獎項。我的父母察覺，這不只是偶然的興趣，因此在中學期間，就鼓勵我要對數學和科學特別用心學習。

我最近才剛從美國回到台灣，希望找到一份工作，能同時報效國家，並運用多年來所學得的知識。我雖然沒有任何工作經驗，但我相信，我的學業成績，能證明我是一個穩重踏實、勤勉、富想像力，而且認眞的員工。

** ────────────────

mechanical〔məˈkænɪkḷ〕*adj.* 機械的
engineering〔ˌɛndʒəˈnɪrɪŋ〕*n.* 工程學
master's 碩士學位（= *master's degree*）
exhibit〔ɪgˈzɪbɪt〕*v.* 表現；顯示
fascination〔ˌfæsṇˈeʃən〕*n.* 強烈的愛好；著迷
ready-made〔ˈrɛdɪˈmed〕*adj.* 現成的
fair〔fɛr〕*n.* 展覽會　　record〔ˈrɛkɚd〕*n.* 成績；記錄
earnest〔ˈɝnɪst〕*adj.* 認眞的

中文簡歷表範例

欄位	內容
姓名	陳正盟
年齡	26
血型	B
性別	男
籍貫	台灣省嘉義縣
通訊處	台北市信義路二段69號3F
電話	(02) 2707-1413
學歷	中山大學企管系畢
經歷	中山大學企管學會會長 哈佛企管顧問公司實習
貼相片	

中、英文履歷表範例

履歷表

欄位	內容
姓名	劉琦芊
年齡	24歲 民國67年5月23日生
性別	女
籍貫	台灣彰化
身份證字號	N225475324
通訊處	台北市安順街72巷18號3樓
電話	(02)2707143
永久住址	彰化市中華路32號
電話	(04)7577392
健康情形	良好
血型	O
身高	157公分
體重	50公斤
學歷	彰化市民生國小 彰化市彰安國中 彰化市彰化女中 清華大學電機工程學系
經歷（或自述）	彰安國中樂隊隊長 彰化女中儀隊隊長 清華大學電子研究社社長 歌林電器公司助理工程員 華亞電腦公司電腦維修實習員
特長	電腦硬體維修、電腦程式設計
應徵職務	電子工程師
希望待遇	三萬二千元起
供食宿	是
	否 √
備註	
貼相片處	

姓名 Name	Lin Tien-teh	性別 Sex	Male	血型 Bloodtype	B
出生日期 Birth Date	Jan. 1, 1982	體重 Weight	120 lb.	身高 Height	5 ft. 6 in.
籍貫 Native Place	Tainan City, Taiwan	已婚 Married		未婚 Single	√
現在地址 Present Address	76 Fusing S. Rd., Taipei				
永久地址 Permanent Address	Same as Above				
學歷 Academic Degree	Bachelor of Mechanical Engineering from the National Taiwan University				
志趣 Pleasures	Reading PC Home, swimming and jogging	專長 Specialty	Mechanical Design	健康情形 Health Condition	Excellent
經歷 Experience	Worked as a mechanic in an engine manufacturing plant during summer vacations (2001–2003)				
簡要自傳 Synoptical Autobiography	I was born and raised for my first five years in Tainan, Taiwan. My mother died in 1986, so my father moved our family to Taipei, to be closer to relatives. My aunt became my and my brother's surrogate mother. I received all of my formal education at Taipei's finest schools, and have consistently been a top student.	相片 Photograph			

English Resume Example
英文履歷表範例

Name: Li Chung-hsing	Gender: (√) Male ( ) Female	
ID Number (for non-Taiwan resident, please fill Passport No.): K226457815		
Birthdate (mm/dd/yyyy): 07/01/1976		
Birth Place: Taipei City		
Height (cm): 178 cm		Attach photograph taken within past 6 months.
Weight (kg): 76 kg		
Blood Type: O		
Marital Status: Single		
E-mail: Eric0701@sina.com.tw		
Current Salary: NT$ 28,000		
Military Status: I completed my military service on June 2001.		
Desired Working Status: (√) Full-time ( ) Part-time ( ) High-level manager		
Handicapped: ( ) Yes (√) No	Nationality: R.O.C.	
※Contact Information:		
1.Mobile Phone: 0938614521	2.Pager:	
3.Fax: 02-29846184	4.Office: 02-26487513	
Preferred Time to Contact: 7 am～10 pm		
Available Date for Next Job (mm/dd/yyyy): August, 2003		
Mailing Address: 56, Anhe Rd., Sec. 2, Taipei		
Permanent Address: same as above		
Main Method of Transportation: (√) Motorcycle ( ) Car ( ) Bicycle ( ) MRT		
Career Level: (√) Full-time ( ) Just Graduated ( ) Part-time Study Daytime ( ) Part-time Study Nighttime ( ) Homemaker ( ) Over Age 40		
Current Career Status: ( ) Employed (√) Between Jobs		

Desired Location to Work (at most 6 choices):
1. Taipei 2. Tainan 3. Kaohsiung
4.____ 5.____ 6.____

Desired Salary (NT$/month): NT$ 28,000

Desired Working Time: from 8 am, to 5 pm

※Language Fluency (excellent / fair):

Language	Listening	Speaking	Reading	Writing
1.English	excellent	excellent	excellent	excellent
2.Taiwanese	excellent	fair		
3.____				

High Education Level Completed:
( ) High School ( ) College (√) University ( ) Master ( ) Doctorate

Desired Job Title: Office Clerk

Software and Programming Language Proficiency:
Word, Excel, PowerPoint, MS-Office, C, C++, RTOS, LINUX, ARM

Typing Speed: 70 words per minute

Other Talents:

Certificate or License:

※Educational Profile: Completion Date (mm/yyyy): June, 2003

	School	Major
High school	Cheng Kung High School	
College / University	National Taiwan University	Computer Science
Master / Doctorate		

※Family Information:

Relation	Name	Occupation (Company or School)
Father	Li Cheng-an	Mechanic of A.I. Company
Mother	Chen Mei-hwa	Professor of Chengchi University
Sister	Li Hsin-chi	Junior of Chengchi University

※Years of Working Experience: 2 years					
	From (mm/yy)	To (mm/yy)	Title	Company	Company Size (Number of employees)
Now	08/01	06/03	Officer	A.I. Company	150
1					
2					
3					

※Reference:			
Name	Company	Title	Phone or E-mail
Wang Chin-yu	A.I. Company	Manager	0925564824
Lo tu-nai	National Taiwan University	Professor	0956545215

※Autobiography (no more than 200 characters):

** gender〔ˈdʒɛndɚ〕*n.* 性別　　marital〔ˈmærətḷ〕*adj.* 婚姻的

handicapped〔ˈhændɪˌkæpt〕*adj.* 殘障的

nationality〔ˌnæʃənˈælətɪ〕*n.* 國籍

permanent〔ˈpɝmənənt〕*adj.* 永久的

homemaker〔ˈhomˌmekɚ〕*n.* 家庭主婦

proficiency〔prəˈfɪʃənsɪ〕*n.* 精通

certificate〔sɚˈtɪfəkɪt〕*n.* 證書　　license〔ˈlaɪsṇs〕*n.* 執照

profile〔ˈproˌfaɪl〕*n.* 簡介

reference〔ˈrɛfərəns〕*n.* 身分證明人；徵信人

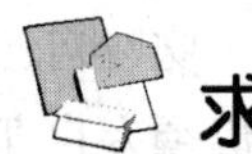

求職信函面面觀

內容用語面

1. 履歷表是你給僱主的第一印象，所以相當重要。在科技當道的世代，請儘量避免手寫履歷，也不要購買市面上的制式履歷表，最好親自或託人以電腦打字、排版、列印，可以給人專業清新的印象。

2. 抬頭儘可能列明公司名稱，或收信人姓氏，不要只寫「敬啓者」，這樣會像是由專業人士代筆。

3. 對收信人的稱呼，應只寫對方的姓氏而不帶名字，並加上專稱（例如博士或教授等頭銜）以示尊敬，要注意職稱不可弄錯。

4. 在第一段就要開宗明義，說明應徵消息的來源，這一段要寫得明確有力，因爲它可能是僱主唯一會仔細看的部分，當然也是你能否獲得面試機會的關鍵。

5. 文中必須突顯自己的資歷及背景，說明自己符合應徵職位的哪些條件，例如在應徵電腦程式員的例子中，便要將自己在電腦方面的才能、專業證照全數列出，以吸引僱主的注意。

6. 對於剛畢業又缺乏工作經驗的人來說，履歷表不但是一篇個人資料，更是推銷利器，所以要盡量突出較優良的學業成績。

7. 不要忽視任何社團或課外活動，從這裡可以反映出你的性格、技能及專長，有助僱主對你進行全面的剖析，即使是不大起眼的活動，也可能會有所助益。例如，參加籃球隊與電腦程式其實是毫無關係，但這項資料可以證實你是個活躍而合群的人。

8. 介紹自己的背景時，不要誇大其詞，吹噓自己的工作能力，寫一些與事實不符的資料；同時，也毋須妄自菲薄，過分謙卑，因爲這樣會使僱主覺得你缺乏自信，根本不會給予面試機會。簡言之，只要態度誠懇，言之有物便可。

9. 在塡寫工作經驗這一欄，即使只是暑期工讀、兼職，甚至是與申請工作沒有直接關係的工作，也不妨列出，總比繳白卷好。而且不要只列出工作頭銜，還要扼要闡述職務內容，這要不只能使僱主更了解你的能力，也能充實你的履歷。

10. 善用一些有力的字眼來加強語氣，例如精通、熱衷、興趣濃厚等（請參考本書第三篇）。

11. 信中多以對方公司的利益爲出發點，例如強調你一旦加入該公司，會有哪些貢獻；相反地，不要過分強調自己的立場。

12. 薪酬方面，不一定要按徵才廣告的要求列出，因爲錯誤的判斷會令你失去面試機會，不妨留待面試時才透露。

13. 資料固然要詳盡，但太瑣碎的事，或太無關痛癢的事情，如小學成績或家庭狀況，則毋須包括在內。

14. 信函的結尾要加上盼望答覆的語句，可加強誠意。

15. 信件結尾的祝頌語不宜過於文縐縐，例如「敬祝時祺」等傳統用語，對現代人顯得很突兀，若不愼用錯更會貽笑大方，所以只要寫得有禮便可。

16. 若有隨函覆寄學歷或其他證明文件，要清楚列明。

17. 寄出履歷前，除了親自再三複誦斟酌字句外，請至少拜託一位友人代爲檢查，以避免出現錯別字或排版不當的情況。

格式佈局面

1. 內容必須簡短，篇幅大約是一至兩頁 A4 紙就足夠。

2. 加上標題，道明來意，清楚寫明自己所應徵的職位，方便對方閱讀之餘，也有利於存檔紀錄。

3. 內容必須分段清晰，每段需有獨立的主旨，條理分明，扼要精簡。因僱主或人事部可能在一天內收到數百封應徵信，如果你的應徵函冗長不堪，將難逃被淘汰的命運。

4. 段與段之間隔行書寫，每段起首預留空間，會使信件顯得更容易閱讀。

5. 在填寫個人資料時，可先寫固定不變的項目，例如姓名、出生日期等，再寫會隨時變動的項目，例如地址、電話等。

6. 至於學歷的排列，也是先後有序的，大前題是先寫「教育」，再寫「專業資格」。文憑當然要排在證書之前，這樣履歷表才會顯得井然有序。

7. 資料的排列次序，也是一個重要課題，例如對沒有工作經驗的人來說，僱主所看重的，當然是你的教育程度及學業成績，所以在履歷表上不妨把這兩項放在顯眼位置。相反地，若應徵者已有數年的工作經驗，就要把工作經歷放在學業成績之前。

8. 無論是用手寫或是電腦打字，一定要以端正整齊爲原則，應多花時間較正別字或錯漏，否則可能會使印象分數大減。

9. 若欲以親自撰寫履歷的方式，請避免使用鉛筆、紅筆書寫。

10. 信紙信封不要摺皺或有污漬，更不要有其他公司的標記或名稱。

4 Resume 1

Frank Lee
No. 43, Lane 501, Sizang Rd.
Taipei, Taiwan, R.O.C.
TEL : (02) 2627-9506

EDUCATION

1 / 03 – 3 / 03	Attended night courses in advanced computer systems analysis at National Taiwan University.
1999	B.S., Electrical Engineering, National Taiwan University, Taipei.

WORK EXPERIENCE

7 / 01 – 4 / 03	Programmer and Systems Designer, China Computer Inc., Taipei. Design programs for customers' individual needs and match components for complete office computer network systems.
8 / 97 – 6 / 99	Sales Clerk, Bao Shin Supermarket, Taipei. Employed in this part-time capacity throughout my last two years at university.

履歷表範例 1

法蘭克・李
中華民國台灣省台北市西藏路五〇一巷四十三號
電話：(02) 2627-9506

學 歷

1 / 03 – 3 / 03 國立台灣大學高級電腦系統分析夜間課程進修。

1999 台北市國立台灣大學電機工程學學士。

經 歷

7 / 01 – 4 / 03 台北市中國電腦公司程式設計員與系統設計師。專爲客戶個人需求設計程式，以及裝配全套辦公室電腦網路系統的零件。

8 / 97 – 6 / 99 台北寶信超級市場售貨員。這是我大學最後兩年的兼差工作。

ADDITIONAL ACTIVITIES

9 / 98 – 6 / 99 Editor of the free monthly Taiwan Computer World publication, volunteer. Published this primarily as a service to other students of Electrical Engineering throughout Taiwan. It was a non-profit organization that received private grants from local businesses; its purpose was to foster better communication and understanding between the departments and students of electrical engineering in Taiwan.

其他經歷

9/98 – 6/99　擔任免費贈閱的「臺灣電腦世界月刊」志願編輯。該刊物的印行主要是爲了服務全台灣其他主修電機工程學的學生。那是個非營利性的組織，受當地企業的私人資助；其目的在增進台灣電機工程學系所與學生之間的溝通與了解。

** component〔kəm'ponənt〕*n.* 零件
network〔'nɛt,wɜk〕*n.* 網路
capacity〔kə'pæsətɪ〕*n.* 職位
grant〔grænt〕*n.* 贈款；獎助金
foster〔'fɔstɚ〕*v.* 促進；培養

Resume 2

Patrick E. Lan
21 Anhe Road, Taipei
TEL : (02) 2713-1791

OBJECTIVE Position with trading or shipping firm.

EDUCATION

Bachelor of Arts, English, 1996,
University of California, Berkeley, minored in French.

Miami Area Vocational College, 1992 – 93.
Enrolled in computer programming courses.

EMPLOYMENT HISTORY

March, 2000 — January, 2003,
Euroamerican Language Institute
1030 W. 7th St., Los Angeles, CA
Employed as administrator of curriculum. Conducted research of unproved and little-used language-teaching methods; selected or developed all teaching materials used at the Institute.

履歷表範例 2

姓名：派翠克・E・藍
住址：台北市安和路 21 號
電話：(02) 2713-1791

目　　標：　貿易公司，或者航運公司的職務。

學　　歷：

1996 年取得文學士學位，畢業於加州柏克萊大學英文系，輔修法文。

1992 年至 1993 年間，於邁阿密地區職業專校，註册研習電腦程式設計課程。

工作經歷：

2000 年 3 月至 2003 年 1 月，在加州洛杉磯西區，第七街 1030 號的歐美語言中心，擔任課程管理員。指導研究少用且未經驗證的語言教學法；並挑選或研發該中心所使用之所有教材。

October, 1998 — March, 2000
Euroamerican Language Institute
Los Angeles, CA
French and English teacher.
Taught English to foreigners and immigrants and French to American citizens; taught all levels of ability.

August, 1996 — October, 1998
Pacific Translation Services, Inc.
663-01 Bloom Ave., San Francisco, CA
Translated documents and acted as interpreter for French tourists and officials.

OTHER

Translated scientific research documents for Science Weekly, a San Francisco-based research and publishing company.

PERSONAL

Enjoy reading both in French and English, especially science-related books or articles. I am also an avid mountain climber and take pleasure in traveling in Europe.

REFERENCES Available upon request.

1998 年 10 月至 2000 年 3 月，在加州洛杉磯歐美語言中心，擔任法文及英文教師。教外國人及移民者英文，教美國人法文。指導各種程度的學生。

1996 年 8 月至 1998 年 10 月期間，在加州舊金山，布魯姆大道 633-01 號太平洋翻譯社，替法國觀光客和官員翻譯資料及口譯。

其　他：

爲位於舊金山的一家研究暨出版公司的科學週刊翻譯科學研究文件。

個人資料：

喜歡閱讀英文和法文著作，尤其是與科學有關的書籍或文章。此外，我是個登山迷，並且非常喜愛到歐洲旅遊。

查詢資料： 隨時備索。

Resume 3

Name : Wang Ta-ming

Sex : Male

Date of Birth : October 17, 1975

Family Status : Married with two children.

Permanent Address : 50 Jhongsiao E. Road, Sec. 7, Taipei

Present Address : 2F, 35, Ren-ai Road, Section 3, Taipei

Education :

Finished the three-year course at Cheng Kung Senior High School, Taipei in 1993. Graduated from College of Commerce, Chung Hsing University, receiving the degree of Bachelor of Arts in Accounting in 1997. Finished the postgraduate course at the same college, receiving the degree of Master of Accounting in 1999.

Experience :

Joined Wei-sheng Trading Co. Ltd., in April, 2000 and was assigned to the Accounting Division, serving in that position up to this date.

Languages : English, Chinese (Mandarin).

Skills : Computer — Word, Excel

I affirm that the above statements are true and correct in every respect.

Taipei, June 15, 2003

(*Signature*)

履歷表範例 3

姓　　名：王大明

性　　別：男

生　　日：一九七五年十月十七日

家庭狀況：已婚。有兩個小孩。

永久地址：台北市忠孝東路七段五十號

目前地址：台北市仁愛路三段三十五號二樓

學　　歷：

一九九三年畢業於台北市成功高中。

一九九七年中興大學商學院畢業，取得會計學學士學位。

一九九九年完成該學院研究所課程，取得會計學碩士學位。

經　　歷：

二〇〇〇年四月進入偉勝貿易股份有限公司，
任職於會計部迄今。

語言能力：英語、中文（國語）。

技　　能：電腦 — Word，Excel

本人確認以上敘述在各方面均眞實無誤。

二〇〇三年六月十五日，台北

（簽名）

Resume 4

JOHN CHANG
P.O. Box 12-977
Kaohsiung, Taiwan

JOB OBJECTIVE

Position in which I can fully utilize my experience and realize my potential, with advancement opportunities based on performance, preferably in Kaohsiung.

EXPERIENCE

9/00 – 3/02 : Head, Loans Department, Citibank, Taipei Branch

3/99 – 9/00 : Assistant to the Head of the Loans Department, Citibank, Taipei Branch

6/96 – 3/99 : Loans Officer A, Loans Department Citibank, Taipei Branch

1/96 – 6/96 : Loans Officer B, Loans Department Citibank, Taipei Branch

履歷表範例 4

姓　　名：張約翰
通訊住址：台灣省高雄郵政 12-977 號信箱

工作目標

藉由工作的機會，能夠學以致用並發揮潛力，且可依工作表現，獲得升遷機會，工作地點最好在高雄。

工作經驗

9 / 00 – 3 / 02：花旗銀行，台北分行，放款部主任

3 / 99 – 9 / 00：花旗銀行，台北分行，放款部主任助理

6 / 96 – 3 / 99：花旗銀行，台北分行，放款部 A 級職員

1 / 96 – 6 / 96：花旗銀行，台北分行，放款部 B 級職員

ACHIEVEMENTS

Received Citibank's Most Improved Officer award in 1998, shortly after which I was promoted to assistant to the Head of the Loans Department.

SPECIALITIES

Especially adept at the use of MS-Office, Word, Excel and PowerPoint. Also familiar with UNIX system, Shell language and SQL.

EDUCATION

M.B.A., Crestwood State College
Crestwood, Vermont, 1995.
B.S., Tunghai University
Taichung Taiwan, 1992.

工作成就

於 1998 年榮獲花旗銀行最上進工作人員獎，之後不久， 就被升爲放款部主任助理。

專　長

特別精通於使用 MS-Office, Word, Excel 和 PowerPoint。同時還熟諳 UNIX 系統，Shell 語言和 SQL。

學　歷

1995 年，美國佛蒙特州克雷斯伍德州立大學企管碩士。

1992 年，台灣省台中市東海大學理學士。

** advancement〔ədˈvænsmənt〕*n.* 升遷
adept〔əˈdɛpt〕*adj.* 擅長；精通
M.B.A. 企管碩士 (= *Master of Business Administration*)

Resume 5

PERSONAL INFORMATION

Name : Hsu-hsiang Liao

Address : NO. 151, Lane 317, Jhongsiao E. Rd.
Sec. 4, Taipei; TEL：(02) 2309-0411

Birthdate : October 16, 1973

Family : Wife and one son.

EDUCATION

Master of Arts, Indiana Central University,
Department of Sociology, 1988

Bachelor of Arts, Department of History,
Tunghai University, 1984

WORK HISTORY

Advisor to Senior Analyst
Market Survey and Research Industries, Chicago, IL
June 1995 — Dec. 2001

Instructor and Research Lab Head
Department of Sociology, Indiana Central University
Jan. 1990 — June 1995

履歷表範例 5

個人資料：

姓　　名：廖樹祥

住　　址：台北市忠孝東路四段 317 巷 151 號；
電話：(02) 2309-0411

出生日期：1973 年 10 月 16 日

家庭狀況：有太太和一個兒子。

學　　歷

一九八八年，印第安那中央大學社會學碩士

一九八四年，東海大學歷史系學士

工作經歷

一九九五年六月至二○○一年十二月，伊利諾州芝加哥市，市場調查與研究業的高級分析員顧問

一九九○年一月至一九九五年六月，印第安那中央大學社會學系講師及研究實驗室主任

Research Assistant, Department of Sociology,
Indiana Central University
July 1988 — Jan. 1990

FOREIGN LANGUAGES

In addition to my native Taiwanese and Mandarin, I also fluently speak, write and read English and Spanish.

一九八八年七月至一九九〇年一月，印第安那中央大學社會學系研究助理

外語能力

除了我的母語台灣話和國語之外，我也能流利地說、寫和讀英文和西班牙文。

** advisor〔ədˈvaɪzɚ〕*n.* 顧問
instructor〔ɪnˈstrʌktɚ〕*n.* 大學講師
Taiwanese〔ˌtaɪwɑˈniz〕*n.* 台灣人；台語
Mandarin〔ˈmændərɪn〕*n.* 國語

Resume 6

Position Applied For: Economic Counselor / Officer

Name : Nancy C. T. Tsai

Address : 7th Floor, 42, Lane 566, Anhe Rd., Taipei

Date of Birth : January 23, 1957

Nationality : Chinese

Marital Status : Married

Sex : Female

Professional Experience

1990 – 2002 : President, Economic Research Association
Seattle, WA, U.S.A.
Pulled the firm up from near bankruptcy to one of America's leading economic research institutes.

1984 – 1989 : Economic Advisor to the Council for Economic Planning and Development, Taipei, R.O.C.
Led committees and teams of economists in mapping out the long-range economic development of the R.O.C.

履歷表範例 6

應徵職位：經濟顧問 / 高級職員

姓名：南西 C.T. 蔡

住址：台北市安和路 566 巷 42 號 7 樓

生日：一九五七年一月二十三日

國籍：中國

婚姻：已婚

性別：女

<u>工作經歷</u>

1990 – 2002：擔任美國華盛頓州西雅圖，經濟研究協會總裁。
將公司由瀕臨破產的邊緣，提昇爲美國主要的經濟研究機構之一。

1984 – 1989：擔任台北經濟計劃與發展會議的經濟顧問。
帶領由經濟學者們組成的委員會與團隊，規劃出中華民國的長程經濟發展。

Educational Background

Ph.D., Microeconomics, University of Wisconsin, Madison, 1984

M.S., Economics, University of Michigan, Ann Arbor, 1981

B.S., Economics, National Taiwan University, Taipei, 1979

Awards

International Academy of Economics' Ralph Samuels Award, 1996, for greatest contribution in 1995 to the field of microeconomics.

Publications

"Microeconomics for the 21st Century," 672 page book, published in 1990 by URZ Publishing Company, Los Angeles.

教育背景

個體經濟學博士，1984 年畢業於麥迪遜的威斯康辛大學

經濟學碩士，1981 年畢業於安娜堡的密西根大學

經濟學學士，1979 年畢業於台北的國立台灣大學

得　　獎

因 1995 年對個體經濟學領域有極大的貢獻，而獲得 1996 年拉福・山繆國際經濟學會獎

著　　作

二十一世紀的個體經濟學，共 672 頁，於 1990 年由洛杉磯的 URZ 出版公司出版。

** association〔əˌsoʃɪˈeʃən〕*n.* 協會
council〔ˈkaʊnsḷ〕*n.* 會議
committee〔kəˈmɪtɪ〕*n.* 委員會
map out 規劃出　***Ph.D.*** 博士 (= *Doctor of Philosophy*)
microeconomics〔ˌmaɪkrəˌikəˈnɑmɪks〕*n.* 個體經濟學
academy〔əˈkædəmɪ〕*n.* 學會

Resume 7

Allison Langford Patterson, C.P.A.
240 Badger Road
Boston, Massachusetts 02136
(617) 493-2531

Certification

Certified Public Accountant, State of Massachusetts, 1998

Education

Master of Professional Accountancy with concentration in Tax, Brandeis University — Boston, Massachusetts
9 / 94 – 6 / 96

Bachelor of Business Administration in Accounting, Boston University — Boston, Massachusetts
9 / 90 – 6 / 94

Experience

Audit Manager 9 / 01 – 5 / 03
ARMAN, GEDDING, PRESCOTT and SMITH
Boston, Massachusetts

履歷表範例 7

愛麗森・藍佛・帕特森檢定合格會計師
巴傑路 240 號
波士頓，麻薩諸塞州 02136
(617) 493-2531

證　照

一九九八年麻薩諸塞州檢定合格會計師

學　歷

專業會計碩士，專攻稅務，布蘭迪斯大學 — 波士頓，麻薩諸塞州（九四年九月至九六年六月）

企業管理會計學學士，波士頓大學 — 波士頓，麻薩諸塞州（九〇年九月至九四年六月）

經　歷

稽查主任，二〇〇一年九月至二〇〇三年五月，阿爾曼公司，波士頓，麻薩諸塞州

Controller, 10 / 00 — 6 / 01

TRAINING SYSTEMS INC.
Division of National Communications Corp.
Boston, Massachusetts

Senior / Staff Auditor, 6 / 98 — 10 / 00

WILSON, RUSH and FENWICK
Boston, Massachusetts

Research Assistant, 1996 — 1997

Professor T.M. Jansen, Brandeis University, MPA Program

Membership

American Institute of Certified Public Accountants (AICPA)
Massachusetts Society (Boston Chapter) of Certified Public Accountants

Honors

Secretary, Honorary Accounting Society, 1999
Business and Professional Women's Foundation Scholarship, 1996

Personal

Date of Birth: 7 May, 1971
Marital Status: Divorced
Health: Excellent

References upon request.

主計員，二〇〇〇年十月至二〇〇一年六月

訓練系統有限公司，國家傳播部，波士頓，麻薩諸塞州

高級稽查員，九八年六月至二〇〇〇年十月

威爾森・拉什・芬威克公司，波士頓，麻薩諸塞州

研究助理，一九九六年至一九九七年

協助 T.M.詹森教授，布蘭迪斯大學，專業會計學碩士課程

會員資格

美國檢定合格會計師協會（AICPA）
麻薩諸塞州檢定合格會計師協會（波士頓分會）

榮　　譽

榮譽會計學會秘書，一九九九年
職業婦女基金會獎學金，一九九六年

個人資料

生日：一九七一年五月七日
婚姻狀況：離婚
健康情形：甚佳

資料備索。

Resume 8

Jeanette Dubois

Taiwan, R.O.C.	Canada
16, Lane 96, Anhe Rd., Taipei	P.O. Box 21-694
TEL：(02) 2712-7716	Quebec City, Quebec

EMPLOYMENT OBJECTIVE

Editorial position with a publishing company.

EDUCATION

University of Quebec, Quebec	Bachelor of Arts in Linguistics, cum laude, 1995

WORK EXPERIENCE

Travel-Asia Magazine Taipei, R.O.C. Mar. 2001 — the present	Assistant Editor and Writer
The China Post Taipei, R.O.C. Oct. 1999 — Mar. 2001	Writer, Reporter
Calgary Post Alberta, Canada Aug. 1995 — Aug. 1999	Reporter and Calgary, Feature Writer

履歷表範例 8

珍妮特・杜波

中華民國台灣	加拿大
台北市安和路 96 巷 16 號	魁北克省魁北克市
電話：(02) 2712-7716	郵政信箱 21-694 號

就業目標

出版公司的編輯工作。

學　　歷

魁北克省，魁北克大學	語言學學士， 1995 年以優等成績畢業

經　　歷

亞洲旅遊雜誌 中華民國台北市 2001 年 3 月迄今	助理編輯及作家
英文中國郵報 中華民國台北市 1999 年 10 月至 2001 年 3 月	作家，記者
卡加立郵報 加拿大亞伯達省卡加立市 1995 年 8 月至 1999 年 8 月.	記者及專欄作家

LANGUAGES

French, English, German

INTERESTS

Writing, reading, learning languages, and traveling.

REFERENCES FURNISHED UPON REQUEST

語　　言

法文、英文、德文

興　　趣

寫作、閱讀、學習語言和旅行。

參考資料備索

** editorial〔ˌɛdəˈtorɪəl〕*adj.* 編輯的
linguistics〔lɪŋˈgwɪstɪks〕*n.* 語言學
cum laude〔ˈkʌmˈlɔdɪ〕*n.* 以優等成績畢業者
feature〔ˈfitʃɚ〕*n.*（報紙上的）專欄
feature writer 專欄作家
furnish〔ˈfɝnɪʃ〕*v.* 供應

Resume 9

Richard C. T. Wang
4th Floor, 277, Lane 664, Jhongcheng Rd.
Taichung, Taiwan, R.O.C.
TEL : (04) 223-6171
Date of Birth : January 1, 1978
Nationality : Taiwan, R.O.C.
Identification Number : A000000001
Position Sought : Chemical Labs Administrator

Education

Bachelor of Science, Department of Chemical Engineering, University of Idaho, U.S.A., 2000

Work Experience

November, 2001 — May, 2003:
Chemical Engineer, Dow Chemical Laboratories, Medical Compounds Division, Kansas City, Kansas. Involved in discoveries of new chemical compounds now used in prescription drugs sold throughout the world. Detailed summary available upon request.

履歷表範例 9

理查 C.T. 王

中華民國台灣省台中市忠誠路 664 巷 277 號 4 樓

電話：(04) 223-6171

生日：1978 年 1 月 1 日

國籍：中華民國台灣

身分證號碼：A000000001

應徵工作：化學實驗室管理員

學　　歷

理學士，2000 年畢業於美國愛達荷大學化工系

工作經驗

2001 年 11 月至 2003 年 5 月：在堪薩斯州堪薩斯市，擔任道化學實驗室藥物合成部的化學工程師。

參與了新化合物的發現，目前這些用於醫師處方的藥物，已銷售至世界各地。詳細摘要備索。

July, 2000 — October 2001:
Plastics Engineer, Flexiglas Inc.
Santa Monica, CA., U.S.A.
Engineered advanced designs that increased longevity and flexibility of some industrial plastics.

LANGUAGES

Native Mandarin Chinese, English, basic German technical language.

2000 年 7 月至 2001 年 10 月：
美國加州聖塔莫尼卡，芙雷克斯格拉斯公司的塑膠工程師。
策劃先進的設計，以提高一些工業用塑膠的壽命及彈性。

語　　言

中文、英文、基本德文技術用語。

** nationality〔ˌnæʃən'ælətɪ〕*n.* 國籍
identification〔aɪˌdɛntəfə'keʃən〕*n.* 身分證
compound〔'kɑmpaʊnd〕*n.* 合成物
Inc. 公司組織（= *incorporated*）
engineer〔ˌɛndʒə'nɪr〕*v.* 策劃
longevity〔lɑn'dʒɛvətɪ〕*n.* 壽命
technical〔'tɛknɪkḷ〕*adj.* 技術的

Resume 10

Allan W. Tennesano
12 Reed Drive
Portland, Oregon 97229
(503) 340-5000

Objective Agricultural Management
Seeking a position with real career potential in the field of Agricultural Management encompassing farm management, agricultural economic accounting, and related responsibilities.

Education Bachelor of Science in Agricultural Economics, 1998-2000
The University of Oregon at Portland
Minor : Business Administration

St. John's University, 1996 — 1997
St. Cloud, Minnesota
Acted as a volunteer in St. Cloud Hospital.

South Florida University (Tampa), 1994 — 1996.
Worked in a 6-week social work project for Tampa's Reform School.

履歷表範例 10

亞倫 W. 田納沙諾
里德路十二號
波特蘭，奧瑞岡州 97229
(503) 340-5000

目 標　農業管理

尋找農業管理，包括農場管理、農業經濟會計，及相關且眞正具有潛力的職務。

學 歷　農業經濟學理學士，一九九八～二〇〇〇

波特蘭，奧瑞岡大學
副修：企業管理

聖約翰大學，一九九六～一九九八
明尼蘇達州，聖克勞德市
在聖克勞德醫院擔任義工。

南佛羅里達大學（坦帕），一九九四～一九九六。
參與爲坦帕感化院所舉辦的，六週社會工作計畫。

Graduate of Carl Morgan High School, 1994, San Diego

- Vice President of Junior and Senior Classes
- Vice President of Student Council (3 Years)
- Member of Drama Club
- Varsity Baseball, Basketball, Football
- Swimming Team

Courses and Hours

- Farm & Ranch Management (3)
- Agricultural Economics (12)
- Agricultural Policy (3)
- Agricultural Prices (6)
- Land Economics (3)
- International Trade (3)
- Business Management (3)
- Accounting (9)
- Marketing & Finance (9)
- Statistics (12)
- Business Law (9)
- Management Problems (3)
- Animal Science (3)
- Quantitative Analysis (3)
- Speech and Technical Writing (3)

一九九四年，聖地牙哥，卡爾・摩根高中畢業。

・二三年級副主席
・學生會副主席（爲期三年）
・戲劇社社員
・棒球、籃球、橄欖球校隊
・游泳隊

<u>課程及時數</u>

・農場及牧場管理 (3)
・農業經濟學 (12)
・農業政策 (3)
・農業物價 (6)
・土地經濟學 (3)
・國際貿易 (3)
・企業管理 (3)
・會計 (9)
・行銷及財務 (9)
・統計學 (12)
・商事法 (9)
・管理問題 (3)
・動物學 (3)
・定量分析 (3)
・演說與專題寫作 (3)

Languages	Fluent Spanish (reading / writing / speaking)
Experience	Employed since 1 / 01 by Lineman Electronics Company (Portland) as a sales manager.
Personal	Aged 27 (born 1 / 25 / 76). Married in 2002 (no children). Willing to relocate; willing to work overseas. Family background：Father owned a farm producing vegetables and cotton (1975 — 1990); and is presently a college instructor.

References and transcripts available on request.

語　　言	流利的西班牙語（讀 / 寫 / 說）
經　　歷	自二〇〇一年一月起被（波特蘭）萊門電子公司聘爲業務經理。
個人資料	二十七歲（一九七六年一月二十五日生）。 二〇〇二年結婚（無子女）。 願意遷調；願意到國外工作。 家庭背景：父親有一座農場，生產蔬菜及棉花（一九七五至一九九〇年）；目前爲大學講師。

資料及成績單備索。

** encompass〔ɪnˈkʌmpəs〕*v.* 包含
responsibility〔rɪˌspɑnsəˈbɪlətɪ〕*n.* 職務
reform school 感化院　　council〔ˈkaʊnsḷ〕*n.* 會議
varsity〔ˈvɑrsətɪ〕*n.* 校隊　　ranch〔ræntʃ〕*n.* 牧場
quantitative〔ˈkwɑntəˌtetɪv〕*adj.* 定量的
technical〔ˈtɛknɪkḷ〕*adj.* 專門的；專題的
relocate〔riˈloket〕*v.* 遷調

Resume 11

Barry P. Comot

Education :

B.S. Marketing, University of Chicago,
1986; minors: Finance, Statistics

Work Experience :

1999 — 2003: Marketing Manager, Dowdley Co., Dallas Through the use of my dynamic approach to marketing, Dowdley's sales quadrupled during this period.

1995 — 1999: Marketing Assistant Manager Dowdley Co. Gained the respect of my peers by introducing a daring but successful marketing scheme.

1987 — 1995: Haskell Overseas Corporation, Ltd., Pittsburgh
(1987 — 89), Market Analyst
(1989 — 92), Supervisor in charge of Finance
(1992 — 95), Assistant Manager of Finance

Detailed work descriptions, samples and reports enclosed.
References available upon request.

Address: 2001 Dowdley Square Apartments Dallas, Texas, 16415

履歷表範例 11

巴利 P. 卡摩

學　　歷：

1986 年畢業於芝加哥大學行銷學系，輔修財政及統計。

工作經驗：

1999 至 2003 年：擔任達拉斯 Dowdley 公司行銷經理。藉由運用我充滿活力的行銷方式，Dowdley 公司在這段時間，業績成長四倍。

1995 至 1999 年：擔任達拉斯 Dowdley 公司行銷副理。由於引進一項創新且成功的行銷計劃，而獲得公司同仁的敬重。

1987 至 1995 年：在匹茲堡，海斯凱爾海外股份有限公司任職。
1987 — 89 年，擔任市場分析員
1989 — 92 年，擔任財務主任
1992 — 95 年，擔任財務副理

附寄詳細工作解說、樣品及報告。詳細參考資料備索。

連絡住址： Dowdley 廣場公寓 2001 號，達拉斯，德州，16415

5 Application Letter 1

Dear Sir,

After graduating from the National Chengchi University Department of International Trade this summer, I will be seeking employment in the field of international trade, and I write you because your foreign trade offices are quite large and well known. Perhaps you would be kind enough to keep my resume on file and me in mind when you next require new help.

I am young and energetic, only twenty-two, and anxious to get started in foreign trade and acquire some practical experience. Though I have not yet held a job, I feel my college record manifests that I am a good, steady, motivated, and reliable worker. The president of my college, Mr. Cheng Jui-cheng, has said that he would be happy to chat with you about my abilities and character. I am free anytime for an interview. I hope to see you soon.

Sincerely,

Wu Hsin-yi

Wu Hsin-yi

應徵函範例 1

敬啓者：

今年夏天我從國立政治大學國貿系畢業後，將在國際貿易的領域內找份工作。由於貴公司的外貿部門有相當的規模及名氣，所以我寫信給貴公司。也許貴公司願意將我的履歷表存檔，留待將來需要新的人才時，將我列入考慮。

我今年只有二十二歲，年輕而充滿活力，我渴望開始從事外貿工作，以獲得一些實務經驗。雖然我尚無工作經驗，但我的大學成績可以證明，我會是個優秀穩健、積極而且可靠的員工。我的大學校長鄭瑞城先生說，他很樂意和您談談我的能力和品格。我隨時有空面談，希望很快見到您。

吳欣儀　敬上

**

resume〔ˌrɛzuˈme〕*n.* 履歷表
anxious〔ˈæŋkʃəs〕*adj.* 渴望的
manifest〔ˈmænəˌfɛst〕*v.* 證明
steady〔ˈstɛdɪ〕*adj.* 穩健的；可靠的
motivated〔ˈmotəˌvetɪd〕*adj.* 積極的

Application Letter 2

Gentlemen,

Please consider my application for the position of accountant, which you advertised in today's Central Daily News. I am twenty-five years old and have just completed my military service.

I graduated in 2001 from National Taiwan University's Department of Political Science. Although this degree is not directly related to the work I would be doing at your company, I do have more than ten years of experience in accounting, for I kept the books and did the unofficial yearly audit for my father's shipping company while I was growing up. I believe that this experience is much more valuable than a degree.

Please be so kind as to notice my enclosed letters of recommendation from Professors Wang and Liu of the Political Science and History Departments, respectively, of Taiwan University.

I would welcome the opportunity to speak with you in person and demonstrate my accounting skills to you. I look forward to hearing from you.

Sincerely,

Wei Mei-li

Wei Mei-li

應徵函範例 2

敬啓者：

關於貴公司今天刊登在中央日報上的求才廣告，請將我的應徵，列入會計一職的考慮。我今年二十五歲，剛服完兵役。

我在二〇〇一年畢業於國立台灣大學政治系。雖然這個學位和我想在貴公司擔任的工作沒有直接關聯，但我有超過十年的會計經驗，因爲我從小爲我父親的船務公司記帳，並做非正式的年度稽核。我相信這個經驗比學位還珍貴。

請注意我附寄的台大政治系王教授，及歷史系劉教授分別所寫的推薦信。

我會很高興能有機會和您面談，並向您展示我的會計能力。我盼望有您的消息。

魏美莉　敬上

** ———————————

irrelevant〔ɪ'rɛləvənt〕*adj.* 不相關的
books〔bʊks〕*n. pl.* 帳簿
unofficial〔,ʌnə'fɪʃəl〕*adj.* 非正式的
audit〔'ɔdɪt〕*n.* 稽核　　enclose〔ɪn'kloz〕*v.*（隨函）附寄
recommendation〔,rɛkəmɛn'deʃən〕*n.* 推薦信
respectively〔rɪ'spɛktɪvlɪ〕*adv.* 分別地
welcome〔'wɛlkəm〕*v.* 欣然接受　　***in person*** 親自
demonstrate〔'dɛmən,stret〕*v.* 展示

Application Letter 3

Gentlemen,

I would like to apply for the position of editor advertised in today's China Times.

I have had a great deal of experience in editing, beginning with a local newspaper in my native Nantou County in 1999 when I was eighteen. After two years there I entered the military, and was discharged twenty months later. I moved to Taipei in 2003 and found a part-time job editing English for The China Post. At the same time, I was studying full-time in The National Taiwan University's Department of Foreign Languages and Literature. Having just received my bachelor's degree, I am seeking full-time employment.

My English is quite good, and I am very experienced in proofreading, rewriting and creative editing in both English and Chinese. Please contact Mr. C. C. Chou of The China Post to learn more about my work attitude and character. I would be pleased to produce samples of my work. Please inform me when I may present myself for an interview.

Yours truly,

Yeh Ching-huei

Yeh Ching-huei

應徵函範例 3

敬啓者：

我想應徵刊登在今天中國時報的編輯職位。

我有豐富的編輯經驗，開始於一九九九年，當我十八歲時，就擔任家鄉南投縣一份地方報紙的編輯。在那裏工作兩年後，我進入軍隊服役，並於二十個月後退伍。我在二○○三年搬到台北，在台大外文系唸書的同時，還在中國郵報找到一個兼職的英語編輯工作。拿到學士學位之後，我想找全職的工作。

我的英文很好，而且對中英校對、改寫及創作編輯都很有經驗。請和中國郵報的周先生聯繫，以便了解我的工作態度及品性。我很樂意附上我的作品樣本。煩請通知我何時可以前往面談。

葉慶輝　敬上

**——————————

discharge〔dɪsˈtʃɑrdʒ〕*v.* 退伍
proofreading〔ˈprufˌridɪŋ〕*n.* 校對
creative〔krɪˈetɪv〕*adj.* 創作的

Application Letter 4

Dear Sir,

I saw your advertisement for an editor in today's United Daily News and would like you to consider my application for this position.

Writing is a large part of my life, and I write whenever I get the chance. Though I have never had an article or story published, this is not due to any lack of interest or skill. I am happy to say that I have, however, edited others' articles and papers which have been published. I will gladly furnish copies upon your request.

At the moment I am a senior in the Speech Communication Department of Shih Hsin University. I am pleased to say that I have one of the best records of my class. Professor C. S. Wang has given me permission to use his name as a reference. Please contact him if you have any questions you would like to ask about my abilities and character. At the same time, I hope you will call me soon to set up an interview. Thank you for your kind attention.

Sincerely,

Lin Jen-ho

Lin Jen-ho

應徵函範例 4

敬啓者：

我在今天的聯合報上，看到貴公司徵求編輯的廣告，希望你們能將我列入考慮。

寫作在我的生活中，佔很重要的地位，我只要有機會就寫作。雖然我的文章和小說都未曾發表過，但絕非因爲缺乏興趣或寫作技巧所致。不過我很高興可以說，我曾編輯過其他人已發表的文章和論文。如果你想要看看，我很樂意提供複本。

我目前是世新大學口語傳播學系四年級學生，而且很榮幸地，我的成績在班上是名列前茅。王教授答應做我的推薦人，如果你們對於我的能力和品格有任何疑問，請和他聯絡。同時，我希望你們儘快打電話和我約定面談時間。謝謝你們的關照。

林仁和　敬上

**

furnish〔ˈfɝnɪʃ〕*v.* 提供
permission〔pɚˈmɪʃən〕*n.* 許可

Application Letter 5

Dear Sirs,

I wish to present my resume to apply for the secretarial position which you advertised on the 104 Job Bank's website.

As stated on my resume, I have seven years of secretarial experience in addition to having completed a five-year business administration course in National Taipei College of Business. I am well versed in typing (80 wpm) and stenography, and I am proficient in the use of Word and Excel. I am also a skilled communicator, fluent in Mandarin, English and Taiwanese.

I hope that you will find my qualifications satisfactory, as I believe I would be of great service to your firm. I hope to hear your favorable reply soon.

Sincerely,

Chou Chung-min

Chou Chung-min

應徵函範例 5

敬啓者：

由於貴公司在 104 人力銀行網站刊登了求才廣告，所以我提出履歷表，來應徵秘書一職。

誠如我在履歷表中所述，我有七年的秘書工作經驗，加上在國立台北商業技術學院上過五年的企管課程。我精通打字(一分鐘八十個字)和速記，而且擅長使用 Word 與 Excel。我的溝通技巧出色，中、英文和台語都很流利。

希望你會認爲我的資格符合要求，因爲我相信我對貴公司會有很大的幫助。希望能很快接到您圓滿的回覆。

周崇敏　敬上

** ——————————

versed〔vɜst〕*adj.* 精通的
stenography〔stəˈnɑgrəfɪ〕*n.* 速記
proficient〔prəˈfɪʃənt〕*adj.* 精通的
qualifications〔ˌkwɑləfəˈkeʃənz〕*n. pl.* 資格；條件
satisfactory〔ˌsætɪsˈfæktərɪ〕*adj.* 令人滿意的；合乎要求的
favorable〔ˈfevərəbl̩〕*adj.* 有利的；圓滿的

Application Letter 6

Dear Sir,

I wish to apply for the position of administrative assistant which you recently advertised in the Liberty Times as being vacant. Please note that I have enclosed a resume and two letters of recommendation.

I think that I fully meet the qualification you specified in your advertisement — that the applicant have a good command of English. I graduated from National Taipei University's Department of Foreign Languages and Applied Linguistics two years ago. I have continued to study English on my own and with foreign tutors since then. Furthermore, I have worked for the ABC Overseas Trading Corporation in Taipei for one and a half years as their English secretary.

The primary reason for my seeking new employment is that ABC Overseas is too small, and I do not have any opportunity to expand my knowledge. I believe that with my background and good working habits, I can be of great value to your company. Please contact me at your earliest convenience.

Very truly yours,

Lu Ching-ching

Lu Ching-ching

應徵函範例 6

敬啓者：

最近我在自由時報上，看到貴公司所刊登的求才廣告，想應徵空缺的行政助理一職。請留意我隨函附上的履歷表，以及兩封推薦信。

我想我十分符合你們廣告中所要求的資格——應徵者須有良好的英文能力。我兩年前從台北大學應用外語學系畢業，此後不斷自修英文，並向外籍家庭教師學習。此外，我還在台北的 ABC 海外貿易公司，做了一年半的英文秘書。

我想換新工作的主要原因是，ABC 海外貿易公司的規模太小，我沒有機會增廣見聞。相信以我的經歷和良好的工作態度，一定能對貴公司助益良多。如果方便的話，請你們儘快和我連絡。

盧青青　敬上

** ———

administrative〔ədˈmɪnə͵stretɪv〕*adj.* 行政的
recommendation〔͵rɛkəmɛnˈdeʃən〕*n.* 推薦；推薦信
specify〔ˈspɛsə͵faɪ〕*v.* 指定
applicant〔ˈæpləkənt〕*n.* 應徵者
command〔kəˈmænd〕*n.* 運用自如的能力；精通
linguistics〔lɪŋˈgwɪstɪks〕*n.* 語言學
tutor〔ˈtutɚ, ˈtjutɚ〕*n.* 家庭教師

Application Letter 7

Dear Sir,

I believe that I am qualified to fill the position which you advertised in yesterday's Apple Daily.

After graduating from National Chung Cheng University's Department of Finance in 2000, I worked for two years as a sales aide in a small trading company in Tainan. I then moved to Taipei to find a more challenging and wide-ranging job. I have worked at the LEGO Company as an accountant since then, but still wish to put to use and expand my knowledge of what I studied in college : Finance.

Mr. Kenneth Chou, my present employer, knows of my ambitions, and is assisting me in locating a more challenging position. He has offered me a letter of recommendation, which I have enclosed. Please call me at your convenience to set up an interview time. Thank you for your assistance.

Sincerely,

Chen Mei-mei

Chen Mei-mei

應徵函範例 7

敬啓者：

貴公司昨天在蘋果日報上刊登求才廣告，我相信我有資格擔任這項職位。

我在二〇〇〇年畢業於國立中正大學的財務金融學系之後，就在台南的一家小型貿易公司擔任了兩年的業務助理。後來搬到台北，想找一份更具挑戰性，而且範圍更廣的工作。從那時起，我就在樂高公司擔任會計，但我仍希望我在大學所學的財金知識能學以致用。

我現在的老板周先生知道我的抱負，所以他一直協助我，找一份更具挑戰性的工作。我附上的推薦函，就是周先生所提供的。請在方便時，打個電話給我，約定面談時間。謝謝您的幫忙。

陳美美　敬上

** ————————————

qualified〔ˈkwɑlə͵faɪd〕*adj.* 合格的
aide〔ed〕*n.* 助理　ambition〔æmˈbɪʃən〕*n.* 抱負
assist〔əˈsɪst〕*v.* 幫助　locate〔loˈket〕*v.* 找到
recommendation〔͵rɛkəmɛnˈdeʃən〕*n.* 推薦；推薦信

Application Letter 8

Dear Sirs,

Please consider me as an applicant for the position of finance manager which you recently advertised on the National Youth Commission's Website. I am thirty-seven years old with both a good academic background and years of financial management experience.

I graduated in the top ten percent of the Department of Accounting of Taiwan University in 1988 and then worked as a teller at the E. Sun Bank. After only a short period of time I was promoted to the bank's Office of Financial Management as a financial secretary, and then promoted again to the position of chief financial secretary. After eight years with the bank I accepted the position of assistant finance manager with the Asian Development Bank, where I have stayed until the present.

I have several references and letters of recommendation available upon request. I would greatly appreciate a personal interview.

Very truly yours,

Lee Fu-ning

Lee Fu-ning

應徵函範例 8

敬啓者：

關於貴公司最近刊登在青輔會網站上的求才廣告，請將我列入財務經理一職的考慮。我今年三十七歲，有良好的教育背景，及數年的財務管理經驗。

一九八八年，我以名列全系前百分之十的成績，畢業於台灣大學會計系，然後到玉山銀行擔任出納人員。只過了一段很短的時間，我就被升爲銀行金融管理部門的財務秘書，然後再升爲財務秘書長。在玉山銀行工作八年之後，我接下了亞洲開發銀行財務副理一職至今。

如有需要，我可以提供一些資料和推薦函備索。若能安排一次面談，我將會非常感激。

李福寧　敬上

**

website〔ˈwɛbˌsaɪt〕*n.* 網站
applicant〔ˈæpləkənt〕*n.* 應徵者
teller〔ˈtɛlɚ〕*n.* 出納員　　promote〔prəˈmot〕*v.* 升遷
available〔əˈveləbḷ〕*adj.* 可獲得的
upon request 一經要求
appreciate〔əˈpriʃɪˌet〕*v.* 感激

Application Letter 9

Gentlemen,

I ask that you consider me for the executive sales management position in your company that was advertised in this month's Career magazine.

I graduated from Hwa Hsia College of Technology and Commerce in 1984; I summarize my experience following graduation below:

1984—1986

Began as a salesman for Asia Fashions Industry, Inc. and moved quickly into an executive sales position. Duties included sales to overseas and domestic clients and later included organization of a management department.

1986—1990

Promoted to overseas sales director. Served in this capacity for four years. The overseas sales of Asia Fashions Industry were doubled during the period of my leadership.

1990—1997

Transferred to domestic sales management as assistant director. Though this appears to be a demotion, it was actually a promotion, as our domestic sales at that time far outweighed overseas sales, and this new position brought me both a higher salary and esteem.

應徵函範例 9

敬啓者：

關於貴公司刊登在本月份的 Career 雜誌上，所徵求的執行業務管理人員一職，請您考慮錄用我。

我在一九八四年畢業於華夏工商專業學校。我將畢業之後的經歷簡述如下：

1984—1986

一開始是擔任亞洲流行服飾工業公司的售貨員，然後很快就升爲執行業務。工作範圍包括對海外及國內顧客銷售，後來職務範圍還包括一個管理部門組織。

1986—1990

升爲海外業務主任，一共擔任該職務四年。在我領導的這段時間，亞洲流行服飾的海外銷售量倍增。

1990—1997

調爲國內業務副理。雖然看起來好像是降職，但其實是升遷，因爲那時我們的國內業務遠比國外業務重要，而且這個新職位給我帶來較高的薪水和評價。

1997—2003

Director of sales, overseas and domestic. Having served in this capacity for six years, and having refined Asia Fashions' sales management, I feel it is time for a change of pace.

My experience and successes speak for themselves, but I would like to point out one item, and that is, that I have throughout my career made it a point to keep abreast of developments in all aspects, types, and forms of commerce, of management skills, and of sales techniques.

I am free any weekday afternoon after three o'clock to meet with you for an interview. I hope you will give my application first consideration.

Sincerely,

Lin Lien-fa

Lin Lien-fa

1997—2003

國內外業務經理。我擔任這個職務六年，並著手改善了亞洲流行的業務管理後，我覺得是到了該調整步調的時候了。

雖然我的經驗和成功可以證明我的能力，但我想指出一點，那就是在我的職業生涯中，我一定會使自己跟上商業型態、管理技能，以及銷售技巧的各項發展。

我每星期一到星期五，三點以後都有空，可以和您面談。希望您能優先考慮我的申請。

林連發　敬上

** ——————————————

executive〔ɪg'zækjʊtɪv〕*adj.* 執行的；行政的
Inc. 公司組織（= *incorporated*）
duty〔'djutɪ〕*n.* 職務　double〔'dʌbḷ〕*v.* 倍增
demotion〔dɪ'moʃən〕*n.* 降職
outweigh〔aʊt'we〕*v.* 較…重要
esteem〔ə'stim〕*n.* 敬重　refine〔rɪ'faɪn〕*v.* 改善
pace〔pes〕*n.* 步調　***speak for themselves*** 不言而喻
make it a point to V. 必定
abreast〔ə'brɛst〕*adv.* 並肩
keep abreast of 跟上（時代等）的步調

Application Letter 10

Dear Sir,

I would like to apply for the position of counsel, which you advertised in the Min Sheng Daily as being open.

I am twenty-seven years old, and I graduated from the Soochow University School of Law four years ago, after which I took my present employment as a counsel with the Apeak Company in Taipei. I am seeking new employment because the Apeak Company is transferring to mainland China.

I believe that you will find the enclosed resume and letters of recommendation satisfactory. My only requirement is a minimum salary of NT$28,000. I am certain that if you hire me, you will be happy with my work. Thank you for considering my application; I hope to be hearing from you soon.

Very truly yours,

Su Wei-ling

Su Wei-ling

應徵函範例 10

敬啓者：

我看了您在民生報上登的廣告，想應徵法律顧問的職缺。

我今年二十七歲，四年前畢業於東吳法律系，然後在台北艾皮克公司，擔任目前這個法律顧問的職位。由於艾皮克公司將移往大陸，所以我想找一份新的工作。

我相信隨函附寄的履歷表和推薦函，定能使您滿意。我的唯一要求是，薪資最低爲兩萬八千元。相信如果您雇用我，將會對我的工作表現很滿意。謝謝您將我的應徵列入考慮；希望能很快收到您的回覆。

蘇維玲　敬上

**

counsel〔ˈkaʊnsḷ〕*n.* 法律顧問
mainland〔ˈmen,lænd〕*n.* 大陸；本土
satisfactory〔,sætɪsˈfæktərɪ〕*adj.* 令人滿意的
minimum〔ˈmɪnəməm〕*adj.* 最低的
be happy with 對～滿意

6 Self-recommendation Letter 1

Dear Sirs,

I will complete my master's program in psychology at the University of Chicago this August, and will then be seeking employment in a related field. I believe that I can easily qualify as a research assistant under your esteemed guidance.

Ever since I was a young man I have heard of developments made in behavioral psychology by your research foundation, and in my undergraduate and graduate work I have often studied your research reports, always finding them to be of the highest academic quality. Furthermore, I am particularly interested in behavioral psychology, and believe that I can make valuable contributions to its research. Therefore, I believe I am qualified to work as a member of your research staff.

If at present you do not have any vacancies for which I might be considered, please retain my application on file so that I may be eligible for any later openings. Please notify me at your convenience if you would like further information about my background. Professors Johnson and Lee of the University of Chicago have offered to act as my references, and you may contact them at the university's Psychology Department. Thank you for your interest.

Sincerely,

Wu Li-wei

Wu Li-wei

自薦函範例 1

敬啓者：

我將在今年八月，完成芝加哥大學心理學系的碩士課程，屆時將在相關的領域內找工作。我相信在您值得信賴的指導之下，我很容易就能勝任研究助理一職。

從我年輕的時候，就聽說過你們的研究機構，在行爲心理學方面的發展；在大學和研究所的作業中，我也經常研讀你們的研究報告，而且總是發現這些報告具有最高的學術品質。此外，我對行爲心理學特別感興趣，相信我在這方面的研究會有重要的貢獻。因此，我相信我符合擔任貴機構研究人員的資格。

如果你們現在沒有可以將我列入考慮的職位，請將應徵信函保留存檔，以便往後有任何適合我的空缺。如果需要進一步的背景資料，請在方便的時候通知我。芝加哥大學的約翰生教授和李教授願意做我的推薦人，你們可以在芝加哥大學的心理系聯絡到他們。謝謝您的關心。

吳立偉　敬上

** ——————————

psychology〔saɪˈkɑlədʒɪ〕*n.* 心理學
esteemed〔əˈstimd〕*adj.* 值得信賴的
undergraduate〔ˌʌndɚˈgrædʒuɪt〕*adj.* 大學的
staff〔stæf〕*n.* 全體工作人員　　retain〔rɪˈten〕*v.* 保留
eligible〔ˈɛlɪdʒəbḷ〕*adj.* 適當的

Self-recommendation Letter 2

Dear Sirs,

I have recently heard that you are in need of an experienced factory supervisor. I have over ten years of experience in such work, and in manufacturing processes very similar to yours.

Enclosed are some materials relating to or certifying my experience in a factory supervisory position. I would greatly appreciate an opportunity to personally visit you and see your factory. Please contact me to arrange a time for an interview.

Sincerely yours,

Liu Li-jen

Liu Li-jen

自薦函範例 2

敬啓者：

最近我聽說貴公司需要一位有經驗的工廠主管。我在這方面的工作經驗超過十年，而且其製造程序與貴工廠非常類似。

隨信附上的是有關，或能證明我具備工廠管理經驗的資料。如果有機會親自拜訪並參觀工廠，我將不勝感激。請與我聯絡，以安排時間面試。

劉利仁　敬上

* ———

supervisor〔ˌsjupɚˈvaɪzɚ〕*n.* 主管
certify〔ˈsɝtəˌfaɪ〕*v.* 證明
supervisory〔ˌsupɚˈvaɪzərɪ〕*adj.* 管理者的
personally〔ˈpɝsn̩l̩ɪ〕*adv.* 親自地

Self-recommendation Letter 3

Gentlemen,

I am a doctoral student in the Biology Department of the University of Alabama, due to receive my degree in just a few months.

I am a Chinese, native of Taiwan, Republic of China, but have lived in the United States now for six years, so my English is nearly as fluent as my Chinese.

I have long admired your company, and have often hoped that I could someday work for you. I believe that your biological research laboratories are the finest in the country.

I received my B.S. from the Biology Department of National Taiwan University in 1995, and then began serving my military service. Upon being discharged in early 1997 I came to the United States and earned my M.S. in biology in 2000 from Louisiana State University (LSU). I then immediately began work on my Ph.D.

自薦函範例 3

敬啓者：

我是阿拉巴馬州立大學生物系的博士班學生，預定再過幾個月之後拿到學位。

我是中國人，在中華民國台灣出生，但是至今我已在美國住了六年，所以我的英文幾乎和中文一樣流利。

我長久以來都對貴公司十分景仰，而且經常希望有一天能爲你們工作。我相信你們的生物研究室是全國最完善的。

我一九九五年拿到台大生物系的學士學位之後，開始服兵役。一九九七年初一退伍，就來美國，在二〇〇〇年拿到路易斯安那州立大學的生物學碩士。之後，立刻開始爲博士學位努力。

Professors Lanen and Douglas of LSU and Professors Kirikin, Theodostore and Serle of the University of Alabama have expressed their wishes to act as my references. They can be reached at the biology departments of their respective universities.

If you have a position available, I would appreciate your considering me for it. If you do not have anything available now, please keep my name on file, as I truly wish to work for your company. Thank you for your kind assistance.

Very truly yours,

Wang Ming-yuan

Wang Ming-yuan

路易斯安那大學的 Lanen 和 Douglas 教授，以及阿拉巴馬大學的 Kirikin，Theodostore 和 Serle 教授，願意做我的推薦人。您可以分別在他們所屬大學的生物系，與他們取得聯繫。

如果你們有空缺的職位，我會很感激你們將我列入考慮；如果目前沒有空缺，請將我的名字保留在檔案上，因爲我眞的很想爲貴公司工作。謝謝您仁慈的幫忙。

王明遠　敬上

** ―――――――――――――――

doctoral〔ˈdɑktərəl〕*adj.* 博士的
due〔dju〕*adj.* 預定的
native〔ˈnetɪv〕*n.* 生於…的人
fluent〔ˈfluənt〕*adj.* 流利的
discharge〔dɪsˈtʃɑrdʒ〕*v.* 使退伍
work on 致力於
reference〔ˈrɛfərəns〕*n.* 可供查問的人；保證人
respective〔rɪˈspɛktɪv〕*adj.* 個別的
assistance〔əˈsɪstəns〕*n.* 幫助

7 Letter of Recommendation 1

Dear Sir,

It is my great pleasure to recommend Miss Lin to you, as she was one of the finest students that I have seen pass through the doors of this department.

Miss Lin began attending classes in the Department of International Trade here in 1999 and graduated in the spring of 2003. Though it has been over three years since I last saw her, the deep impression she made on me has not faded in the least. As she was in my class when a senior, I was able to become well acquainted with her, and found her not only to be highly intelligent, but also courteous, honest and sincere as well. Her high academic achievement speaks for itself: she consistently scored in the top 10% of her class.

Miss Lin would be worth far more to any organization than the salary she would be paid. I highly recommend her for the position you have open. Please contact me again if I may be of further service.

Very truly yours,

Chen Hsiao-hsun

Chen Hsiao-hsun

Chairman, Department of

International Trade

National Taiwan University

推薦函範例 1

敬啓者：

我很高興能向您推薦林小姐，因爲就我所知，她是本系最優秀的畢業生之一。

林小姐於一九九九年開始進入國貿系就讀，且畢業於二〇〇三年春天。雖然距離我上次見到她，已經有三年多的時間，但她給我的深刻印象，卻一點也沒有消失。由於她在大四那年修我的課，所以我才有機會能與她更加熟識，並發現她不僅非常聰明，而且有禮貌，正直又誠懇。她在學業上的優秀表現是顯而易見的：她的成績一直維持在班上的前百分之十以內。

林小姐値得任何公司高薪聘用，我極力推薦，由她來擔任貴公司空缺的職位。如果需要我提供更多協助，請再與我連絡。

陳曉勳　敬上
台灣大學國貿系主任

** ———————————

not the least 一點也沒有　　fade〔fed〕*v.* 消失
courteous〔ˈkɜtɪəs〕*adj.* 有禮貌的
speak for itself 顯而易見
consistently〔kənˈsɪstəntlɪ〕*adv.* 始終不變地
score〔skor〕*v.* 得分　　further〔ˈfɜðɚ〕*adj.* 更進一步的
chairman〔ˈtʃɛrmən〕*n.* 主席

Letter of Recommendation 2

Dear Sir,

Thank you for your inquiry concerning Mr. Chao. I am certain that you will find that he is well worth your efforts.

Mr. Chao and I have been acquainted now for over six years, since 1997, when he enrolled in the National Taiwan University's Department of Mathematics, of which I am a professor. Throughout his four years at Taiwan University Mr. Chao displayed outstanding academic abilities as well as fine character. He is quick to learn, but unlike many of this type, he does not become bored with a task or assignment when he has mastered it.

Upon his graduation in 2001, Mr. Chao took a job with the HG Computer Company. I met a manager of the company not too long ago, and he informed me that Mr. Chao is the finest mathematician among their staff. I was not surprised at all.

I feel that Mr. Chao would make a fine addition to your staff, so I highly recommend him for the job. Please do not hesitate to inquire further if I can be of help to you.

Sincerely,

Wang Hsi-ting

Wang Hsi-ting

推薦函範例 2

敬啓者：

謝謝您詢問我有關周先生的事。我確信您將發現他是一個值得您爭取的人才。

自從一九九七年，周先生進入我所任敎的國立台灣大學數學系至今，我們認識已經超過六年了。周先生在台灣大學的四年中，品學兼優。他的學習能力強，但在熟悉一項工作或作業之後，卻不像其他人一樣會感到厭煩。

周先生在二〇〇一年畢業後，就到恆鉅電腦公司工作。我不久之前遇到那家公司的經理，他告訴我，周先生是他們的職員中，最優秀的數學家，我一點也不驚訝。

我覺得周先生能使貴公司的員工陣容更強大，所以我極力向您推薦他。如果您還需要我幫忙的話，請儘管問，不要猶豫。

王希定　敬上

** ──────────

inquiry〔ˈɪnkwərɪ〕*n.* 詢問　enroll〔ɪnˈrol〕*v.* 入學
enroll in 進入　display〔dɪˈsple〕*v.* 展示；顯露
outstanding〔ˈaʊtˈstændɪŋ〕*adj.* 傑出的
academic〔ˌækəˈdɛmɪk〕*adj.* 學術的
master〔ˈmæstɚ〕*v.* 精通　***not…at all*** 一點也不
addition〔əˈdɪʃən〕*n.* 附加物；增加物
hesitate〔ˈhɛzəˌtet〕*v.* 猶豫

Letter of Recommendation 3

Gentlemen,

I am more than happy to comply with your request for information regarding Mr. Lu Ying-sheng. I am pleased that you have this opportunity to gain the allegiance of such a bright young man.

Mr. Lu and I have been like family ever since he came to work for my company in 1990, when he was only fourteen years old. His father had recently died, and he had to help financially support his younger brothers and sisters, a task he still attends to today. He worked six hours each day after school, and during those four years I never heard him complain once. Furthermore, he often volunteered to work overtime. What is most impressive about this is that he still managed to maintain excellent grades throughout high school.

After his graduation from National Tsing Hus University in 2002 he took a job with the 3M Corporation as a chemical engineer. I've spoken with his supervisor, Mr. William Anders, several times. He has always told me how bright and industrious Mr. Lu is. He also added that Mr. Lu's cheerful attitude had contributed to a general rise in morale.

I am certain that Mr. Lu would make great contributions to your company, and I strongly recommend him for the position. Please contact me again if I can be of any service.

Sincerely,

Nieh Chi-hsin

推薦函範例 3

敬啓者：

我非常樂意答應你們的請求，提供有關盧穎昇先生的資料。你們有機會請到這麼聰明的年輕人來效勞，我替你們感到高興。

自從盧先生一九九〇年到我的公司工作開始，他和我一直就像是一家人，他當時只有十四歲，父親剛過世，所以他必須在經濟上資助他的弟妹，至今他仍努力完成這項任務。他每天放學後工作六小時，而且在那四年裏，我從沒聽他抱怨過。此外，他時常自願加班。最令人印象深刻的是，他在高中時代，一直設法維持著優秀的成績。

他於二〇〇二年從國立清華大學畢業後，就在 3M 公司找到一份化學工程師的工作。我跟他的主管，威廉・安德斯先生聊過幾次，他總是告訴我盧先生有多聰明、多勤勉。他還說盧先生愉快的工作態度，使得公司的士氣普遍提升。

我確信盧先生會對貴公司有重大的貢獻，我極力推薦他擔任這個職位。如果還有我幫得上忙的地方，請和我聯絡。

聶紀信　敬上

** ──────────

comply〔kəm'plaɪ〕*v.* 順從
allegiance〔ə'lidʒəns〕*n.* 效忠　***attend to*** 努力
impressive〔ɪm'prɛsɪv〕*adj.* 令人印象深刻的
morale〔mo'ræl〕*n.* 士氣

8 Certificate of Service 1

Feng Lung Industries
Certificate of Service

July 31, 2003

Miss Kao Yu-wen began working at Feng Lung Industries as a receptionist on November 20, 1996. She was promoted to assistant secretary on June 10, 1997, and to secretary to the vice president on January 22, 1999, in which position she remained until her resignation on July 31, 2003.

Miss Kao is an efficient and reliable person. During her years at Feng Lung she never ceased to impress us with the fine quality of her work. Most impressive was her ability to take charge in emergencies.

Liao Shu-tze
Liao Shu-tze
Personnel Department

經歷證明書範例 1

芬 隆 工 業 公 司

經 歷 證 明 書

2003 年 7 月 31 日

高郁文小姐從 1996 年 11 月 20 日開始，在芬隆工業公司擔任接待人員。1997 年 6 月 10 日升爲助理秘書，然後又在 1999 年 1 月 22 日，升爲副總裁的秘書，她一直擔任這個職位，直到 2003 年 7 月 31 日辭職爲止。

高小姐是個工作有效率而且可靠的人。在爲芬隆公司工作的這幾年間，她一直都以良好的工作表現，使我們印象深刻。最令人難忘的是，她處理緊急事件的能力。

人 事 部
廖 述 資

** ——————————

receptionist〔rɪˈsɛpʃənɪst〕*n.* 接待人員
resignation〔ˌrɛzɪgˈneʃən〕*n.* 辭職
efficient〔əˈfɪʃənt〕*adj.* 有效率的
cease〔sis〕*v.* 停止
personnel〔ˌpɝsṇˈɛl〕*adj.* 人事的

Certificate of Service 2

Lai Wang, Inc.
Certificate of Service

April 21, 2003

Mr. Lee Ta-hsiung joined this company as the assistant manager of the Export Department on March 1, 2001. He was promoted to manager of the same department six months later, and worked in this capacity until he resigned on April 15, 2003.

He is remembered here for his cool-headed approach to problems and silent industry. He was well liked and highly respected.

Chang Ching-li
Chang Ching-li
President

經歷證明書範例 2

雷 王 有 限 公 司
經 歷 證 明 書

2003 年 4 月 21 日

李大雄先生於 2001 年 3 月 1 日進入本公司，擔任出口部副理。六個月後，他升為該部門的經理，並且擔任這項職務直到 2003 年 4 月 15 日辭職為止。

他以冷靜的方法處理問題，並默默地努力工作，讓人印象深刻。他很受愛戴和尊敬。

總　　裁
張 青 立

** ———

capacity〔kə'pæsətɪ〕*n.* 職位
cool-headed〔'kul'hɛdɪd〕*adj.* 頭腦冷靜的
approach〔ə'protʃ〕*n.* 方法
industry〔'ɪndəstrɪ〕*n.* 勤勉

Certificate of Service 3

Universal Trading Co., Ltd.
Certificate of Service

June 1, 2003

This is to certify that Miss Wu Tai-an entered this company as a salesperson on August 24, 1999. She was promoted to the position of sales manager on March 1, 2001, in which capacity she remained until she resigned on February 15, 2003.

Miss Wu made great contributions to the organization of this office. Under her supervision our business dealings increased by a large margin. Moreover, she is a model character who always treated others with dignity and respect, no matter their position.

Lo Chi-cheng
Lo Chi-cheng
General Manager

經歷證明書範例 3

萬國貿易有限公司
經歷證明書

2003 年 6 月 1 日

茲證明，吳苔安小姐於 1999 年 8 月 24 日，進入本公司擔任業務員。2001 年 3 月 1 日晉升爲業務經理，並擔任該職位到 2003 年 2 月 15 日辭職爲止。

吳小姐對本公司的體制貢獻良多。在她的監督之下，本公司的業務量大幅成長。此外，她是個模範人物，因爲不論對方的職務爲何，她總是以尊重的態度來對待別人。

總 經 理
羅 奇 錚

**

certify〔ˈsɝtə,faɪ〕*v.* 證明
salesperson〔ˈselz,pɝsn̩〕*n.* 售貨員
organization〔,ɔrgənəˈzeʃən〕*n.* 組織；體制
supervision〔,supɚˈvɪʒən〕*n.* 管理
margin〔ˈmɑrdʒɪn〕*n.* 幅度
character〔ˈkærɪktɚ〕*n.* 人物
dignity〔ˈdɪgnətɪ〕*n.* 尊嚴
general manager 總經理

9 Certificate of Release 1

Wan Shan Architectural Engineers, Inc.
Certificate of Release

March 31, 2003

This is to certify that Ms. Yan Ning-mei was hired by this company as a drafter on January 15, 1998. She was promoted on November 30, 1999, to assistant design engineer, and again on January, 2000, to design engineer. She was employed here until her resignation, effective April 30, 2003. Ms. Yan was hardworking, honest and upstanding. Her work here always exceeded expectations.

Yang Min-chong
Yang Min-chong
Chairman

離職證明書範例 1

萬山建築工程有限公司
離職證明書

2003 年 3 月 31 日

茲證明，楊寧美小姐於 1998 年 1 月 15 日起，受聘於本公司，擔任製圖員一職。她於 1999 年 11 月 30 日，晉升爲助理設計工程師，2000 年 1 月，再升爲設計工程師。她在此任職直到 2003 年 4 月 30 日，辭職生效爲止。楊小姐工作認眞，爲人旣誠實又正直。她在這裡的工作表現總是出乎意料的好。

董事長
楊明樣

**

release〔rɪ'lis〕*n.* 離職
drafter〔'dræftɚ〕*n.* 製圖員
effective〔ɪ'fɛktɪv〕*adj.* 生效的
upstanding〔ʌp'stændɪŋ〕*adj.* 正直的
expectation〔ˌɛkspɛk'teʃən〕*n.* 期望
chairman〔'tʃɛrmən〕*n.* 主席

Certificate of Release 2

ASUSTEK COMPUTER INC.

Certificate of Release

December 30, 2003

Miss Feng Yi-mei was hired on July 1, 2000 as a secretary and worked here until December 19, 2003, when she resigned her position. She was punctual, trustworthy, and dependable.

Shen Tien-lin

Shen Tien-lin

General Manager

離職證明書範例 2

華碩電腦股份有限公司

離職證明書

2003 年 12 月 30 日

方怡美小姐在 2000 年 7 月 1 日受雇爲秘書，然後在本公司一直工作到 2003 年 12 月 19 日辭職爲止。她很守時、值得信任，而且可靠。

總 經 理

沈 添 麟

** ―――――――――――――――

punctual〔ˈpʌŋktʃuəl〕*adj.* 守時的

trustworthy〔ˈtrʌstˌwɝðɪ〕*adj.* 值得信任的

Certificate of Release 3

Paramount Sporting Goods
Certificate of Release

This is to certify that Mr. John Lai was employed as a sales executive at Paramount for the period beginning May 1, 1998 and ending October 30, 2003, when he resigned. Mr. Lai is an upstanding young man of great abilities and energy.

Lin Shi-ching
Lin Shi-ching
Manager, Sales Department

離職證明書範例 3

派拉蒙運動用品公司

離職證明書

茲證明，賴約翰先生受聘爲派拉蒙公司的業務主管，從1998年5月1日起，到2003年10月30日辭職爲止。賴先生是個很有能力，並且有衝勁，而且又正直的青年。

業務部經理

林 喜 清

**

goods〔gʊdz〕*n. pl.* 商品

executive〔ɪgˈzækjʊtɪv〕*n.* 主管

10 Letter of Employment 1

Business Bank of Barcelona

Certificate of Employment

This certifies the employment of Mr. Markus Florenzo as a bank teller in our establishment, effective July 1, 2003.

Carlos Estrada

Carlos Estrada

Bank Manager

聘書範例 1

巴塞隆納商業銀行
聘　書

茲聘請馬爾庫斯・弗羅倫索先生爲本銀行出納員，於 2003 年 7 月 1 日起生效。

此　聘

銀行經理
卡爾羅斯・艾斯德拉達

**

teller〔'tɛlɚ〕*n.* 出納員
establishment〔ə'stæblɪʃmənt〕*n.* 公司
effective〔ə'fɛktɪv〕*adj.* 生效的

Letter of Employment 2

Fast Lane Trading Company

Certificate of Employment

This certifies that Liu Shi-ming was employed by the Fast Lane Trading Co. on September 9, 2003 as an inspector.

Wang Wei-kang

Wang Wei-kang

President

聘書範例 2

快線貿易公司

聘　書

茲於 2003 年 9 月 9 日聘請劉希明，擔任快線貿易公司檢查員。

此　聘

董事長

王維康

** ———

inspector〔ɪn'spɛktɚ〕*n.* 檢查員

president〔'prɛzədənt〕*n.* 總裁；董事長

Letter of Employment 3

Export Associates
Certificate of Employment

Export Associates of Taipei hired Chen Chin-yu as manager of the Shipping Department on November 12, 2003, at a starting salary of $42,000.

Hsieh Tsu-ting
Hsieh Tsu-ting
General Manager

聘書範例 3

外銷合作社

聘　書

台北外銷合作社於 2003 年 11 月 12 日，聘請陳慶餘擔任運輸部門經理，起薪爲四萬二千元整。

此　聘

總 經 理

謝 祖 定

**

shipping〔'ʃɪpɪŋ〕*n.* 運輸

associate〔ə'soʃɪˌet〕*n.* 合作社

11 求職前的準備工作

有許多人對甫從學校畢業，準備踏入社會的新鮮人持有負面評價，認爲七年級生們幾乎都是草莓族，外表光鮮亮麗，其實不堪一擊。在這樣的負面輿論包圍下，縱使有滿腹才幹，也不容易找到眞正適合的工作。再加上現在景氣低迷，就業機會嚴重縮水，如何找到一份好工作，已經是全民最關心的熱門話題。

俗話說：「工欲善其事，必先利其器。」想找一份好工作，就得在求職前做好萬全的準備，才能搶得先機。

既然目標是找到適合自己的好工作，當然得先認清自己。所以，第一步就是仔細想想，自己有沒有哪一方面的天賦超人一等，例如：反應敏捷、思慮縝密，或是耐力十足等。第二步是要找出自己的興趣，例如對數字特別敏感，或是對文字撰稿方面特別在行。第三步是分析自己的個性，要知道自己究竟是屬於沉穩內向，還是活潑外向的人。如果是沉穩內向的人，或許可以從事文書或編輯型的工作；反之，如果是活撥外向的人，不妨考慮業務方面或接待人員的工作。

第四步是列出自己的專業能力，譬如擅長使用電腦，或是精通英文。專長通常都和所學密不可分，但若能發展第二技能，將對找工作有莫大的助益。第五步是檢測自己的身體狀況，身強體壯的人可以選擇工時不固定，或需要在外奔波的工作；但身體狀況較不強健的人，則可能需要選擇勞心，或工時固定的工作。當然這並非定論，但雇主通常會將健康情形列入考慮，因爲它對工作表現有一定程度的影響。

第六步是找出適合自己性別的工作，雖然現代社會強調男女平等，但是有些需要大量體力的工作，對女性而言的確較難勝任；相反地，服務性質高的工作，則以女性的柔和特質較爲適合。最後一步是考量自己的年齡，年輕人應該找比較具有發展性的工作，替未來鋪路，但是也不要刻意避免短期雇員性質的工作，因爲這樣總比失業好，況且可以藉這個機會磨練一下自己，還可以趁機學習該行業的專業知識。

接下來，就是利用各種管道，找出所有產業的特質。爲了因應目前一職難求的窘境，政府和私人機關都分別提供了許多徵才的媒和服務（詳見本書第三篇），求職者只要來電或上網查詢，很快就能夠了解各行業所需求的特質。大體而言，業務方面的工作需要親和力與說服力；行政方面的工作需要細心與耐心；公務人員是服從爲負責之本；軍警人員需強健的體魄和敏捷的反應；而設計人員需要創意和坦然接受失敗的心胸。

充份瞭解各個行業的特質之後，再拿出之前的自我分析結果，就可以馬上找出比較適合自己的工作。當然工作不光是靠特質即可成就的，幾乎每一份工作，雇主都會加上一些條件設限，像是需要有相關工作經歷，或是必須具備某方面的技能。此時，不妨考慮參加一些訓練學習課程，來提升自己的競爭力，這樣才能確保勝券在握。

以上所談的都是關於如何找到工作的方法，畢竟這是一個人求事的時代，保險一點的做法，還是得抱持著騎驢找馬的心態，先有一份工作，可以一邊學習，一邊還有固定的收入；然後再充實自己，才比較有可能找到理想的好工作。至於如何分辨哪些才是好工作，以下提供幾點建議，讀者可用來檢視自己的工作。

1. 管理開明。一家朝令夕改的公司，容易讓員工感到無所適從，天天忙著抱怨都來不及了，哪有心思努力求上進。

2. 福利完善。唯有這樣的環境能讓員工的權益不至於受損，當然並不是說一定要每年分紅幾十萬，但基本的勞健保和年假則是不可或缺的。

3. 工時固定。現代人注重休閒品質，講求工作時要拼命，休息時當然也要完全的放鬆。固定的上下班時間，有助於增進工作效率。

4. 薪資合理。合理的薪資才能讓員工覺得努力有所回報，公司整體才能共同向上。

5. 最理想的好工作是能學以致用的工作。在自己熟悉的領域，通常都能有最穩定出色的表現。

6. 企業形象良好。良好的企業形象一般而言都代表著，公司的制度完善可靠，在這樣的環境下，員工才有本錢不顧一切地往前衝。

7. 產業前景光明。放眼今日，面臨倒閉或裁員的產業，絕大多數都是傳統製造業或加工業。反之，服務業和電子科技業則眞是人人搶破頭的鐵飯碗。光明的產業前景意味著工作多一層保障。

8. 員工訓練完備。總括而言，幾乎是大型公司較有能力提供完整的員工訓練或進修管道，這是最理想的狀態。但小型公司的員工也無須忿忿不平，因爲小型公司人力缺乏，常常拿一個人當三個人用，在先天不良的條件下，員工通常反而能學到更多實務面的經驗，這是任何員工訓練都教不來的。

9. 升遷制度明朗公平。明朗而公平的升遷制度，才能讓員工找到努力的目標，也才有動力爲公司打拚。

10. 工作環境清新。所謂清新的工作環境，就是說同事之間的互動良好，不會爲了公事或私事而勾心鬥角，甚至互相中傷，俗話說：「團結力量大」，公司整體要有最突出的表現，畢竟還是要靠員工同心協力來達成。

最後要提醒讀者的是，要注意無所不在的求職陷阱，凡是工作內容模糊，或連絡方式僅列出電話號碼，連公司名稱地址都沒寫清楚的，通常都是比較可能出問題的工作環境。

再者，如果讀者即將加入直銷或傳銷公司，務必要在徵詢長輩的意見後多加考慮。因爲一般的直銷或傳銷公司，都是需要先繳一定的會員費，買下固定數量的產品，然後自行將產品推銷給別人，並從中獲利。聽起來並不難，但是加入這樣的行業，還沒賺錢就得先花錢投資，再說向別人推銷，更不是件容易的事。親朋好友可能有人樂意購買，也可能是勉爲其難的買你人情；但若是素昧平生的陌生人，怎麼可能輕易把錢掏出來給你呢？

總而言之，天下沒有白吃的午餐，要想找到好工作，一定要花時間認清自己，認清工作，否則再厲害的千里馬也找不到伯樂。

2. Questions You Will Be Asked

面試必問考題

1 應徵英文筆試準備重點

通常大專程度以上的工作，應徵時都會安排一項正式或非正式的筆試（有時視需要加考如打字、操作電腦等技能），筆試之後擇其成績較優者進行面試。因此**筆試成績的好壞，足以影響面試的機會**。

筆試除了專業科目之外，英文幾乎是人人必考的一個科目。其形式與內容完全視該公司及該項工作之需要，因此只要稍加分析，就不難掌握其範圍。

首先必須了解，應徵時的筆試主要是**證實應徵者的實力**。因此題型通常較大衆化，而且便於比較程度。就英文一科來說，最普遍的要算**字彙測驗、翻譯和作文**了。其內容大多爲專業性的範圍，例如貿易公司可能考一些商業術語，和商業文件的翻譯與撰寫；電子公司可能考一些電子零件、產品、電腦知識的翻譯等。所以準備的要領不外乎**熟記該行業的專門用語，以及熟悉各類有關文件、資料的形式與內容**。而且最好在應徵前挑一些內容模擬幾次，因爲筆試題目雖不一定相同，卻必爲類似題。這樣一來，您就可以從容作答，被錄取的機率自然會提高。

最後一定要注意的事項是，作答時千萬記得：不論考什麼科目，**字體力求工整**，切忌潦草與過多的塗改。畢竟，保持美好的「**第一印象**」永遠是最基本的條件！

2 應徵面試成功12要訣

當你十分渴望擁有這份工作時，「面試」就成了最大的考驗。

以面試反敗爲勝！

你相信嗎？很多人的筆試成績平平，但卻在面試這一關奇蹟式的脫穎而出，眞有一套！其實，這是有原因的，因爲面試非常重要，它往往是這家公司決定錄取與否的最後關鍵！

各式各樣的面試！

一般來說，一個有制度的公司要徵才，通常會要求你寄履歷和自傳（或作品）、參加筆試、然後再面對面的「面試」。如果更謹愼的公司，會要求你面試好幾次，如主任面試、經理面試、總經理面試…等等。或者，有些公司在面試時，會請你到一間會議室去，全公司的重要幹部（如董事長、總經理、經理…等）都圍成一圈，對你提出一連串的問題。這時候，你的機智和談吐，便面臨考驗！

換句話說，面試是在「很短的時間內」，讓人與人「面對面」達到溝通效果的一種方式；你如何能在這麼短的時間內，把自己推銷出去？而公司如何能在這麼短的時間內，了解你是否正是他們所需要的人才？並且，他們也會設法讓你相信，這是一家可以讓你發揮長才，一展抱負的公司。

下面我們就來談談，面試成功最重要的 12 項關鍵：

面試前

1. 先收集資料，了解對方！

知己知彼，百戰百勝。面試之前，你應該廣泛收集有關這家公司的一切資料。請注意，這項工作非常重要！首先，你應該了解這家公司的性質（它是哪一種行業？）、他們的業務情況（過去業績好不好？業務往來的對象爲何？）、內部組織、員工福利、一般起薪、未來的工作地點、工作性質…等等。

2. 哪些問題可能被問到？（請參考本書第三篇）

把可能會被問到的問題一一列舉出來：

- 先請你自我介紹。
- 你來本公司應徵的原因。
- 你的工作能力如何？專業知識有多少？
- 曾在哪家公司任職？爲何離職？

⋮

然後，先以自問自答的方式練習幾次，或商請親友幫忙模擬面試情境，這樣可以提高臨場面試的成功率，事先有所預習，也就能對答如流、不慌不亂了。

3. 認識自己的性向

以上談的，都是一些如何「很有技巧地」做好面試的準備工作。其實還有一項十分重要，那就是——了解你自己的志趣。在求職之前，要好好想一想：自己眞正追求的目標是什麼？自己的人格適合從事哪一種行業？自己的能力到底有多少？

這樣，當你求職時，就不會人云亦云地盲目追求，最後投錯行，或方向偏差了！

面試當天

4. 一定要守時。最好早到10分鐘左右。太早到達會讓應徵公司措手不及；太晚到達則給人不專業的印象。
5. 服裝儀容應該依你所應徵的行業，或工作的性質，而稍加修飾。一般的面試官多半在面談開始70秒內，即決定是否錄用該名應徵者，故面試時的穿著打扮非常重要。社會新鮮人無須故做成熟打扮，但亦不可著牛仔褲前往面試，整體應以整潔莊重爲要。
6. 言談舉止要自然，說話要誠懇而有自信。
7. 態度積極熱心，表示自己對這份工作非常有興趣。
8. 注意禮貌，如進門之前先敲門，結束後須道謝。
9. 坐姿要端正，眼睛自然地直視對方。
10. 心情保持輕鬆，面帶微笑。答話時要穩健、有條理、有系統，並且避免重覆。不要中途打斷主試者的話，注意傾聽比說更重要。
11. 適當提出問題，但勿直接詢問薪資或私人問題。若主試官問及薪資要求，可回答依公司規定，或提出一合理範圍，例如25000~28000元之間，儘量不要設限爲一定金額。
12. 面談結束後，你可以主動與面試官握手致謝，或寫一封簡短的致謝函，以表明對這份工作的喜愛。也許會因此讓對方對你的印象更好，而大大提高你被錄用的機會呢！

3 求職秘訣▸面試衣著篇

所謂「佛要金裝、人要衣裝」，如何讓面試官第一眼便覺得，你就是他所尋找的千里馬呢？首先，你得讓自己看起來像該行業的專業人士。無論男女，穿出自信與風格都是最重要的。另外，走路要抬頭挺胸，切記，充滿自信的人最有魅力。

男生方面，較適合新鮮人的打扮爲西裝、襯衫，西裝以深色系爲主。襯衫有兩種選擇，八字領給人穩重感，尖領給人幹練的感覺，而顏色則以白色及藍色最適合。至於領帶，是對整體造型最具畫龍點睛效果的部分，以絲質最能表現個人質感，花色則勿過度誇張即可。最後是皮鞋與公事包，皮鞋需樣式簡單、表面清潔，但不可搭配白色或鮮豔色的襪子。公事包則只要大小適中就沒問題了。

女生方面，須穿出現代感，上半身以白色或粉色系襯衫、針織衫爲主，下半身則可搭配深色長褲或及膝裙。髮型以簡單整齊爲首要，髮色不宜過度漂染。彩妝部分，以自然淡雅最佳，濃妝豔抹或脂粉不施皆不合宜。面試時穿的鞋子以中低跟的包頭鞋最適合，新鞋或鞋跟過高都容易加深不自在感，影響面試表現。此外，穿著絲襪爲基本禮儀。配件方面，避免會發出聲音的首飾，應選用金、銀或珍珠材質的，方能給人高雅的感覺。最後要注意的是，手提包以一個爲限，尺寸不宜過大。

求職時不妨依照應徵職務調整穿著，高科技產業須打扮樸素而不失幹練，傳播業須展現個人風格，廣告行銷業須時髦有創意，服務業須有好氣色與親和力，金融業則須兼具優雅與穩重氣質。最後，出門前一定要在鏡子前面，從頭到腳檢視一遍，以免功虧一簣。

1. Personal Information
詢問個人資料

面試者： What is your name, please?
= Your name, please.
= Please give me your name.
= May I have your name?
請問你叫什麼名字？

應徵者： My name is Huang Li-min.
= I am Huang Li-min.
我的名字是黃立民。

面試者： Where were you born?
你在哪裡出生？

應徵者： (I was born) In Taipei.
（我在）台北（出生的）。

面試者： Where are you living now?
你現在住在哪裡？

應徵者： I am living at 71, Jhongshan N. Rd., Sec. 6, Taipei.
我住在台北市中山北路 6 段 71 號。

面試者： How old are you?
= May I ask your age?
= What is your age?
你今年幾歲？

應徵者： I am twenty-four.
我今年二十四歲。

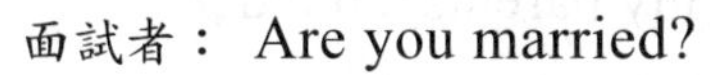

面試者： Are you married?
你結婚了嗎？

應徵者： No, I'm single. 不，我單身。

Yes, I'm married. 是的，我已婚。

面試者： Do you have any religion preference?
你有任何宗教信仰嗎？

應徵者： Yes, I'm a Christian. 有，我是基督徒。

No, I'm an atheist. 沒有，我是無神論者。

【附註】 Buddhist 〔'budɪst〕 *n.* 佛教徒
Taoist 〔'tauɪst〕 *n.* 道教徒
Muslim 〔'mʌzlɪm〕 *n.* 回教徒

面試者： Have you fulfilled your military service?
你服過兵役了嗎？

應徵者： Yes, I have. 是的，我服過了。

No, I haven't. 不，我還沒服過兵役。

2. Family
詢問家庭狀況

面試者： How many people are there in your family?
你家裡有多少人？

應徵者： We're four in all — my parents, an elder brother and me. My father is a surgeon.
我們家總共有四個人 — 我的父母親、一個哥哥和我。我父親是個外科醫生。

面試者： Where's your family from?
你們是哪裡人？

應徵者： We're from Taoyuan.
我們是桃園人。

面試者： Do you have any brothers and sisters?
你有任何兄弟姊妹嗎？

應徵者： Yes, I have a younger brother and two elder sisters. My sisters are married, and my brother is a college student.
是的，我有一個弟弟、兩個姊姊。我的姊姊都已經結婚了，弟弟是大學生。

面試者： What does your father do?
你的父親從事什麼行業？

應徵者： He is an executive director of a construction company. 他是一家建設公司的常務董事。

面試者： Does your mother have a job?
你的母親有工作嗎？

應徵者： No, she is a housewife.
沒有，她是家庭主婦。

面試者： Would you tell me something about your family?
你能告訴我關於你家裡的一些事情嗎？

應徵者： There are six in my family — my grandmother, my parents, a younger brother, a younger sister, and myself. My father keeps a store. My brother is a university student, and my sister goes to a senior high school. We live in Sindian. We often go on a picnic on the weekend.
我家共有六個人，我祖母、我的父母、一個弟弟、一個妹妹，以及我自己。我爸爸開一家店。弟弟是大學生，妹妹是高中生。我們住在新店。我們週末常去野餐。

3. College
詢問科系及學校

面試者： What school did you graduate from?
你是哪所學校畢業的？

應徵者： I graduated from Fu Jen Catholic University in 2000.
我在 2000 年畢業於輔仁大學。

面試者： Where did you receive your master's degree?
你是在哪裡拿到碩士學位的？

應徵者： From National Taiwan University.
國立台灣大學。

面試者： When did you graduate from the university (graduate school)?
你是何時從大學（研究所）畢業的？

應徵者： I graduated in 2003.
我是 2003 年畢業的。

面試者： Have you received any degrees?
你有拿到任何學位嗎？

應徵者： Yes, I have received both a Bachelor of Arts and a Master of Arts degree in English literature.
有，我有英國文學學士及碩士兩個學位。

面試者： What subject did you major in in university?
在大學時，你主修哪一科？

應徵者： I majored in business administration.
我主修企業管理。

面試者： What was your major in college?
你在大學的主修科目是什麼？

應徵者： My major was chemistry.
我的主修科目是化學。

面試者： Did you engage in any clubs in college?
你大學時曾參加過任何社團嗎？

應徵者： Yes, I was a member of the basketball team.
是的，我曾經是籃球隊的隊員。

4. Grades and Scores
詢問在校成績

面試者： What grades did you get at high school?
你高中時的成績如何？

應徵者： I got an average of 90 points.
我得到平均 90 分的成績。
= I am an A student.
我得到 A 等的成績。【美式説法】

面試者： How were your scores in college?
你大學時成績如何？

應徵者： They were above an average of 85. For the first two years I had to study many general subjects, but I didn't find them very interesting. I didn't work very hard. But in my third year, I started to study major subjects and I worked harder. My scores rose after that.
平均在 85 分以上。前兩年，我必須修許多共同科目，但是我發覺它們不太有趣，所以我不是很用功。但是從第三年起，我開始修專業科目，就比較用功了。我的分數從此開始提高。

面試者： Did you have a good record in English?
你的英文成績好嗎？

應徵者： Yes, I obtained 90 points in English.
是的，我的英文得到九十分。

面試者： What was your favorite subject？ Why?
你最喜愛什麼科目？爲什麼？

應徵者： Marketing Management. This subject was taught in English. I could not only develop an intuition about marketing and systematical thinking, but also improve my English. Of course I learned a lot about how to solve real marketing problems in this course.
我最喜歡行銷管理。這個科目是用英語授課。我不僅能培養行銷方面的直覺和有系統的思考方式，還增進了我的英文程度。當然，我也在這門課學了很多，如何解決實際行銷問題的方法。

Calculus, accounting and algebra were my favorite subjects because I'm good at computing numbers.
微積分、會計和代數是我最愛的科目，因爲我對計算數字很在行。

面試者： What was your worst subject?
你最糟的科目是什麼？

應徵者： Well, that might be calculus. I could never learn to like it very much, so my marks weren't very good. Formulas were hard for me to understand, and in calculus class there were a lot of formulas.
嗯，可能是微積分。我沒辦法學著非常喜歡它，所以我的成績不是很好。公式對我來說是難以理解的，而微積分課卻總是有許多公式。

5. Reasons for Applying
詢問應徵的原因

面試者： Have you ever been employed?

= Do you have any work experience?

你曾經受雇嗎？；你有工作經驗嗎？

應徵者： No, I have no working experience.

不，我沒有工作經驗。

Yes, I worked as an interpreter from July 2001 to June 2003.

是的，我從 2001 年 7 月到 2003 年 6 月，擔任口譯員的工作。

面試者： Do you have any licenses or other special qualifications?

你有任何執照，或是其他特別的資格證明嗎？

應徵者： I have an auto mechanic's license and a driver's license. 我有汽車技工執照和駕照。

面試者： Do you have any certified qualifications or any licenses for skills?

你有任何資格證明，或技術執照嗎？

應徵者： Yes, I have a lawyer's certificate.

= I have a law license.

= I am licensed to practice law.

是的，我有律師執照。

面試者：Could you tell me what made you choose this company?

你能不能告訴我，什麼原因使你選擇本公司？

應徵者：I think working in this company would give me the best chance to use what I have learned in the university. As you may know, I majored in genetic engineering. They say the prospects for genetic engineering are very bright, and this company is leading this field. So I want to be a part of this company.

我認爲在貴公司工作，能給予我學以致用的最佳機會。正如你所知，我主修基因工程學。據說基因工程學的前途非常看好，而貴公司又在這個領域居領先的地位。所以我想要成爲貴公司的一員。

面試者：Tell me what you know about our company.

告訴我任何你所知道的，有關我們公司的事。

應徵者：Well, the company is the third largest machine tool producer in the world. It was founded in New York in 1975. I know the company has been making efforts to develop new robots since last year.

嗯，貴公司是全世界第三大機械工具製造商。1975 年成立於紐約。我知道貴公司從去年開始，就致力於研發新型的機械人。

面試者：Why are you interested in working with this firm?
你爲什麼對在本公司工作感興趣？

應徵者：I've been interested in computers since high school, when I even wrote a few simple programs. I majored in computer program design in university. Your company is one of the largest computer companies in the world, and I wish to have the opportunity to apply my knowledge working here.
我從高中就對電腦很感興趣，當時我還自己寫了一些簡單的程式。我大學時主修電腦程式設計。貴公司是全世界最大的電腦公司之一，所以我希望能有機會在這裡工作，運用我在這方面的知識。

面試者：What is your most significant achievement?
你最重要的成就是什麼？

應徵者：I successfully planned the graduation party for 500 people when I was a junior in college. And almost every participant appreciated it.
我大三時成功地籌劃了五百人的畢業舞會。幾乎每個參加舞會的人，都給予很高的評價。

My most significant achievement is that I directed a group of 15, and made my last company's sales increase by 50%.
我最大的成就是，曾領導一個十五人的團體，並使前公司的銷售額增加了百分之五十。

面試者： Why did you pick this organization?
你爲什麼選上我們這個機構？

應徵者： Well, I've cherished a desire to get a job where I can use my English, and then I saw your company's advertisement. It looked really interesting. I think your company has a bright future, and I'd be able to develop my capabilities here, if given a chance. That's why I applied.
嗯，我一直希望能找到使用英語的工作，後來我看到貴公司的廣告。它看起來眞的很有趣。我認爲貴公司的前途光明，如果給我機會，我便能在貴公司一展長才。這就是我來應徵的原因。

Well, I've heard a great deal about this company from a friend of mine who works here. And I'm very interested in industrial design, and I'm sure I can do good work for you. There is another point. I like traveling. If I am employed by this company, I'll have many opportunities to travel to foreign countries, I think.
嗯，我從在這邊工作的朋友那裡，得知許多關於貴公司的事。我對工業設計很有興趣，而且我確定，我能將工作做好。還有另外一點，我喜歡旅行。如果我被貴公司錄用，我想我將有許多到國外旅遊的機會。

面試者： Have you done any work in this field?
你曾做過這一行的工作嗎？

應徵者： Yes. Since 1999 I've been employed as a clerk in the Taipei Branch of the ABC Trading Crop.
是的，從 1999 年起，我就在 ABC 貿易公司台北分公司當職員。

面試者： Your personal history says you've been working at the Golden Financing Company for the past two years. Why do you want to change jobs?
你的個人資料上說，你過去兩年一直在戈登財務公司工作。你為什麼要換工作呢？

應徵者： Yes, that's right. The work given to me is rather dull. I want to develop my abilities in a large company like this.
是的，那是正確的。我的工作相當枯燥乏味。我希望能待在像貴公司這樣大的機構，以培養自己的能力。

面試者： According to your resume, you have had some experience working in a foreign company. May I ask why you left?
根據你的履歷表，你有在外國公司工作的經驗。請問，你為什麼離職呢？

應徵者： Yes. I worked at the Peak International Engineering Company for two years. I left, however, because the job was not challenging enough.
是的，我在皮克國際工程公司工作了兩年。而我離職的原因是，那份工作不夠有挑戰性。

面試者： Why do you plan to change your job?
你為什麼打算換工作？

應徵者： Because I think the salary is not equal to my work.
因為我認為薪水和工作不相等。

面試者： Why do you think we should employ you?
你認爲我們爲何應該要雇用你？

應徵者： I am the proper person for this position, not only because I'm good at analysis, but also because I have worked in this field for over ten years. I'm sure that my professional ability can be of great help to your company.
我是擔任這個職務的適當人選，不只是因爲我擅長分析，而且也因爲我待在這個領域，已經超過十年了。我很肯定，以我的專業能力，必能對貴公司大有助益。

面試者： If we employ you, what section would you like to work in?
如果我們錄用你，你會選擇在哪個部門工作？

應徵者： If possible, I'd like to work in the international department.
如果可能的話，我希望在國際部門工作。

面試者： What starting salary would you expect?
你希望起薪多少？

應徵者： I'd like to start at about $25,000 a month.
我希望起薪是每個月兩萬五千元。

面試者： Tell me what you think a job is.
告訴我，你認爲工作是什麼。

應徵者： Well, a way to make a living, of course, but beyond that it's a way of developing as a person.
嗯，當然是一種求生存的方式。但除此之外，工作也是一種使人成長的方式。

面試者： What are your long-term goals?

你的長期目標爲何？

應徵者： I would like to be promoted to a sales manager in about three to five years. With my work potential, I believe that I will be ready for the position by that time.

我希望再過三到五年後，可以升爲業務經理。相信以我的工作潛力，屆時我將能準備好接任這個職位。

面試者： What does a job mean to you?

工作對你而言，有什麼意義？

應徵者： I think a job is another kind of life style. The most important thing is to seek achievement and to enjoy yourself at work.

我認爲工作是另一種生活方式。最重要的，就是要追求成就和樂在工作。

面試者： Is there anything particular that you would like the company to take into consideration?

你有任何特別條件，需要本公司列入考慮的嗎？

應徵者： No, nothing in particular.

不，沒什麼特別條件。

6. Foreign Language Abilities
詢問外語能力

面試者： How is your language ability?
你的語言能力如何？

應徵者： I'm sure that I can easily handle daily situations in English. Besides English, I can speak Chinese Mandarin, Taiwanese and French.
我確定我可以輕鬆地用英語應付日常情況。除了英語，我還會說國語、台語，和法語。

面試者： Do you think you are proficient in both written and spoken English?
你認爲自己精通英語的說和寫嗎？

應徵者： Yes, I think I am quite proficient in both written and spoken English.
是的，我認爲我對英語的說和寫兩方面都很在行。

面試者： You would be using mainly English in this job. Can you manage English conversation?
這份工作主要是使用英語。你能應付英語會話嗎？

應徵者： Yes, I am sure I can.
是的，我確定我能。

面試者：Do you think you can make yourself understood in English with ease?
你認爲你能輕鬆地用英語表達嗎？

應徵者：Yes, I think I can in ordinary circumstances.
是的，我認爲在一般情況下，我可以。

面試者：Do you think you speak English quite fluently? Tell me about your English education.
你認爲你的英語說得很流利嗎？告訴我有關你的英語教育。

應徵者：Yes, I think I speak English quite fluently. I got a high score on the TOFEL and I majored in English in college.
是的，我認爲我的英語說得相當流利。我的托福成績很高，而且在大學時，我主修英語。

面試者：Please tell me about your English learning.
請告訴我你學習英語的情形。

應徵者：I have been studying English since junior high school. I'm listening to Studio Classroom every day. I had good opportunities to practice English conversation when I visited California last year.
我從國中開始學英文。每天都收聽空中英語教室。去年我到加州去時，有了一些練習英語會話的好機會。

面試者： Employees in this company have to have a good command of English. Have you studied English conversation?

本公司的職員必須具備良好的英語能力。你學過英語會話嗎？

應徵者： Yes, I have been studying English conversation since high school. I attended Liu-yi Learn School's "One Breath English Class" this summer. Now I'm sure that I have really mastered English.

是的，我從高中以來，就一直在學英語會話。今年夏天，我還參加了劉毅英文的「一口氣英語班」。現在，我肯定自己十分精通英語。

I think I speak English fairly fluently. I have been attending an evening course in English conversation for four years. And I often read books and magazines in English.

我認為我的英文說得相當流利。我在一家夜間英語會話班上了四年的課。而且我時常閱讀英文書籍和雜誌。

面試者： One of the most important things for this job is English proficiency. Do you speak English fluently?

精通英文是這份工作最重要的一點。你的英語說得很流利嗎？

應徵者： Yes, I think I do. I have often explained historical places in Taiwan to foreign tourists in English. They say my English is quite good.

是的，我認為是。我常用英文向外國觀光客解說台灣的古蹟。他們說我的英文很棒。

7. Personality and Hobbies
詢問個性及嗜好

面試者：What kinds of sports do you like? And do you watch or play?
你喜歡什麼樣的運動？你是觀賞還是運動？

應徵者：I like tennis and mountain climbing. I enjoy both playing and watching. I was in the climbing club all through school.
我喜歡打網球和登山。我喜歡親自去參與，以及觀賞這些運動。在學校時，我一直都參加登山社。

面試者：How do you spend your free time?
你如何打發空閒時間？

應徵者：I usually read, go swimming, or go shopping. I run or play tennis or do something else like that to get some exercise to keep fit.
我通常閱讀、游泳，或者去逛街。我利用跑步、打網球，或做其他類似的運動，來保持健康。

面試者：Do you have any people you'd call really close friends?
你有沒有稱得上是知己的朋友？

應徵者：Yes, but they've all moved to distant places, and we rarely get together. So we keep in contact through letters and phone calls.
有，但是他們都搬到遙遠的地方去了，我們很少聚在一起。所以我們都用寫信或打電話來保持聯絡。

面試者： Are you introverted or extroverted?

你的個性內向或外向？

應徵者： I wouldn't call myself extroverted. Sometimes I enjoy being by myself very much. But other times I like sharing activities with others, too.

我不認爲自己外向。我有時候很喜歡獨自一個人。但有些時候，也喜歡跟其他人一起從事一些活動。

I'm rather outgoing, I think. I enjoy mixing and doing things with others.

我認爲自己相當外向。我喜歡和別人交往，並且一起做事。

面試者： What kind of personality do you think you have?

你認爲你的個性如何？

應徵者： Well, I approach things very enthusiastically, I think, and I don't like to leave something half done. It makes me nervous — I can't concentrate on something else until the first thing is finished.

嗯，我想我會很熱衷於處理事情，我不喜歡做事情做一半，那樣會使我緊張——在第一件事情完成之後，我才有辦法集中精神做其他的事。

面試者： What do you think is the most important thing you need to be happy?

對你來說，使你快樂的最重要因素是什麼？

應徵者： For me, this would be having good relationships with my family members. My family has always been very close-knit, and we still spend a lot of time together. We all depend upon one another for moral support, and without that I would be much less happy than I am.

對我來說，快樂是來自和家人之間的良好關係。我的家人一直都很親近，但我們仍然花很多時間相處。我們在精神上互相支持，如果沒有他們的支持，我就不會像現在那麼快樂了。

面試者： What motivates you the most?

什麼東西最能激勵你？

應徵者： I am mostly motivated by a sense of responsibility. If my superior requests me to undertake a task, I will try my best to do my work well.

我最常被責任感所激勵。如果我的上司要求我負責一項工作，我就會儘可能地把工作做好。

I'm mostly motivated by the fact that my talent and specialty can be put to good use. If I have a chance to exercise my ability, I will feel satisfied. Even if I fail at last, I'll still know that at least I have had a full and fruitful life.

大多數的時候，若能充分利用自己的才能和專長，我就會很有動力。如果我有機會運用自己的能力，我就會感到滿足。即使最後失敗了，我還是會明白，至少我擁有充實而豐富的人生。

面試者： Could you please describe yourself?
能請你形容一下自己嗎？

應徵者： I'm creative and industrious. I'm good at communicating with people and persuading others. I'm now looking for challenging employment in a well established company.
我有創意而且勤勉。我擅長和人們溝通，並說服別人。目前想在一家深具規模的公司，找具有挑戰性的工作。

面試者： What do you think are your strongest skills?
你認爲自己最強的技能是什麼？

應徵者： My strongest skills are listening and solving problems with great patience and composure. Without these skills, I think people can't handle emergencies well.
我最強的技能，就是以極大的耐心和冷靜的態度，來傾聽並解決問題。如果沒有這些技能，我想人們會無法處理緊急情況。

面試者： What do you think are your greatest strengths and weaknesses? 你認爲自己最大的優點和缺點爲何？

應徵者： Being a perfectionist is both my greatest strength and my greatest weakness. It is my strength because I always try my best to do my work well. It is my weakness because I am sometimes reluctant to delegate responsibility to others.
身爲一個完美主義者，是我最大的優點，也是最大的缺點。因爲我總是會盡力把我的工作做好，所以這是我的優點。但我有時候會不願意把責任交付給其他人，所以這也是我的缺點。

8. The End of the Interview
結束面談

面試者： How can we contact you about our decision?
我們如何把結果通知你呢？

應徵者： You can call me at this number between four and six in the afternoon.
你可以在下午四點到六點，打這個電話給我。

面試者： May I call you at your home about our final decision?
我能打電話到你家，通知你最後的決定嗎？

應徵者： Yes, please. My telephone number is 2707-1413. 可以。我的電話號碼是 2707-1413。

面試者： Shall we notify you of our decision by telephone, or by mail?
我們應該以電話，還是信件通知你我們的決定？

應徵者： By telephone, please. Do you have my number?
請以電話的方式。你有我的電話號碼嗎？

面試者： We'll get in touch with you by next Wednesday. Thank you for coming.
我們會在下星期三以前，和你聯絡。謝謝你來面試。

應徵者： Thank you, Mr. Parker.
謝謝你，派克先生。

面試者：Thank you for your interest in this job.
謝謝你對這份工作感興趣。

應徵者：Thank you, sir (or ma'am). Good-bye.
先生（或女士），謝謝你。再見。

面試者：Thank you, Mr. Kim, for your interest in our company. Good luck to you.
謝謝你對我們公司感興趣，金先生。祝你好運。

應徵者：Thank you, Mr. Carter. 卡特先生，謝謝你。

面試者：You'll be hearing from us. Send the next applicant in on your way out, please.
你將會接到我們的消息的。出去時，麻煩請下一位應徵者進來。

應徵者：Certainly. Thank you very much.
好的。非常感謝你。

面試者：It has been pleasant talking with you.
很高興能和你談話。

應徵者：I've enjoyed talking with you, too. Thank you.
我也很高興和你談話，謝謝。

面試者： The interview is over. Now you might leave.
面談已經結束，你現在可以離開了。

應徵者： Thank you very much.
非常謝謝你。

面試者： That's enough. You may leave now.
這樣就夠了。你現在可以離開了。

應徵者： Thanks a lot.
多謝。

面試者： Good. That's all for now. You may go.
好。今天就談到這裡。你可以走了。

應徵者： Thank you very much, sir. Good-bye.
非常謝謝你，先生。再見。

面試者： Thank you for coming, Miss Lee. It was nice talking to you.
謝謝妳來面試，李小姐。和妳談話眞愉快。

應徵者： Thank you. Mr. Foster.
福斯特先生，謝謝你。

3. English Conversation for the Interview

面試實況會話

1. Clerk in Trading Company

Mr. Lin's friend has told him of a job opportunity at the trading company where he works. Mr. Lin has come for an interview with the manager, Robert Clark.

應徵者： Good morning.

面試者： Sit down, please.

應徵者： Thank you.

面試者： You are Mr. Lin Wei-hsin? I'm Robert Clark.

應徵者： Yes. Nice to meet you, Mr. Clark.

面試者： What's your present address?

應徵者： 36, Lane 450, Min-sheng East Road, Sec.3, Taipei.

面試者： Are you married?

應徵者： No, I'm single.

面試者： Tell me about your education, please.

應徵者： I graduated from National Taipei University two years ago, and I majored in commerce, with an emphasis on foreign trade.

1. 應徵貿易公司職員

林先生的朋友告訴林先生，在他服務的貿易公司，有個工作機會。林先生前來和經理羅勃·克拉克面談。

應徵者：早安。
面試者：請坐。
應徵者：謝謝。

面試者：你是林偉新先生嗎？我是羅伯·克拉克。
應徵者：是的，很高興見到你，克拉克先生。

面試者：你目前住在哪裡？
應徵者：台北市民生東路三段 450 巷 36 號。

面試者：你結婚了嗎？
應徵者：不，我目前單身。

面試者：請告訴我，你的教育程度。
應徵者：我兩年前畢業於國立台北大學，主修貿易，尤其是國際貿易。

面試者：How fast is your key-in skill?

應徵者：I can type 50 words a minute.

面試者：I see by your resume that you are working for a trading company. May I ask how long have you been working at that company and why you want to change jobs?

應徵者：I have been working there for three years. I want to change jobs because that job is lacking in challenge. Also, the salary is too low.

面試者：You may know that Taiwan is trying hard to enter the WTO and WHO. What do WTO and WHO stand for?

應徵者：WTO stands for "World Trade Organization," a kind of world trade administrative institution. And WHO stands for "World Health Organization." The WHO's goal is the attainment by all peoples of the highest possible level of health.

面試者：What will be different after Taiwan gets into the WTO?

應徵者：After Taiwan gets into the WTO, we should reduce our tariffs step by step. We have to give some members Most Favored Nation status. At the same time, we must open our services and market to all WTO's members.

面試者：你打字速度有多快？

應徵者：我每分鐘能打五十個字。

面試者：我從你的履歷表得知，你目前正在一家貿易公司工作。我可以請教你，你在那家公司做多久，還有你爲什麼要換工作嗎？

應徵者：我已經在那邊工作三年了。我想換工作的原因是，那份工作缺乏挑戰性，而且薪水太低了。

面試者：你可能知道台灣正在努力加入 WTO 和 WHO。那 WTO 和 WHO 各代表什麼？

應徵者：WTO 是「世界貿易組織」，它是一個世界貿易管理機構。而 WHO 是「世界衛生組織」。WHO 的目標是使全人類的衛生條件達到最高水準。

面試者：台灣加入 WTO 之後，會有什麼不同？

應徵者：在台灣加入 WTO 之後，我們應該會一步一步地降低關稅。台灣還必須給其他會員國「最惠國待遇」。同時，我們必須開放服務業和市場，給所有 WTO 的會員。

面試者：What made you choose this company?

應徵者：A friend of mine works here, and he told me about your company, so I became interested. I think working in this company would provide me with a good opportunity to use my knowledge.

面試者：What do you know about this company?

應徵者：This company was established in New York in 1965 and is one of the biggest trading companies, with a capital of 50 million dollars. It employs more than 10,000 throughout the world. A Taiwan branch was established ten years ago.

面試者：Have you applied at any other foreign companies?

應徵者：Yes, I have applied at the ABC Trading Corporation. That company is smaller than this company, but the work is very similar.

面試者：I see. By the way, would you describe yourself as outgoing or introverted?

應徵者：I'm not really sure — maybe partly both. I'd rather cooperate with everybody else and get the job done by working together.

面試者：Can you name one person that you respect very much?

應徵者：Mm… Dr. Martin Luther King. He impressed me with the way he worked for Black liberation and equality. His "I Have a Dream" speech has had a big effect on me. I've listened to the tape of that speech many times.

面試者：你爲什麼選我們這家公司？

應徵者：我有一個朋友在這裡工作，他告訴我有關貴公司的事，所以我很感興趣。我想在這家公司工作，也許可以提供我運用自己知識的好機會。

面試者：你對我們這家公司了解多少？

應徵者：貴公司是世界上最大的貿易公司之一。1965 年成立於紐約，資本額是五千萬美元。它在世界各地所僱用的職員超過一萬人。十年前成立了台灣分公司。

面試者：你有應徵其他外商公司嗎？

應徵者：有，我曾去 ABC 貿易公司應徵。那家公司比貴公司小，但工作內容很相似。

面試者：我明白了。順便一提，你認爲自己是外向還是內向？

應徵者：我不太確定 —— 也許兩者都有一點。我喜歡和大家合作，然後一起把工作完成。

面試者：你能說出一位你非常尊敬的人嗎？

應徵者：嗯…馬丁・路德・金恩博士。他對黑人解放與平等所做的努力，使我大受感動。他那篇「我有一個夢」的演講，對我產生很大的影響。我已經聽過很多遍那場演講的錄音帶了。

面試者：What kinds of sports do you like?

應徵者：I like bowling. I also like watching baseball and boxing matches.

面試者：You didn't ask, but you'd want to know about the salary. The starting salary for clerks in the Trade Department is 25,000 dollars a month, and raises are given after six months according to your ability. We provide fringe benefits such as semi-annual bonuses, three weeks paid vacation a year, and health insurance. Is this satisfactory?

應徵者：Yes, it's quite satisfactory.

面試者：Any questions about the job?

應徵者：I heard that some of your Chinese employees are sent to the United States to attend the training program offered by the head office of the firm. I'd like to know how you choose employees for the program.

面試者：Almost all Chinese employees are eligible for the training course, but as the number of trainees at one time is limited, we select them by their merits.

應徵者：One more question. Are there chances for Chinese employees to be transferred to the head office in New York or other branch offices around the world?

面試者：你喜歡什麼運動？

應徵者：我喜歡保齡球，還喜歡看棒球和拳擊比賽。

面試者：你沒有問，但我認為你會想知道薪水方面的事。貿易部職員的起薪是每個月兩萬五千元，六個月後，再根據你的能力加薪。我們提供額外福利，像一年發兩次獎金，每年有三星期的給薪休假，還有健保。這些你還滿意嗎？

應徵者：是的，這些令人很滿意。

面試者：有任何關於這個工作的問題嗎？

應徵者：我聽說你們有一些中國職員被送往美國，去參加由總公司提供的訓練課程。我想知道你們如何挑選接受訓練的職員。

面試者：幾乎所有中國職員都有資格參加訓練課程。但是由於每一次的受訓名額有限，我們只好依照他們的業績來選擇。

應徵者：還有一個問題是，中國職員有沒有機會被調往紐約的總公司，或其他位於世界各地的分公司呢？

面試者：Certainly. There would be a good chance for you to work overseas, I think. How about the job? Are you interested?

應徵者：Sure. I'll do my best if I become a part of this firm.

面試者：It has been pleasant talking with you, Mr. Lin. We'll notify you of our final decision by next Monday.

應徵者：Thank you, Mr. Clark. Good-bye.

面試者：Good-bye.

面試者：當然有。我想你應該很有機會到國外工作。這個工作如何？你有興趣嗎？

應徵者：當然。如果我成爲貴公司的一員，我將會全力以赴。

面試者：和你談話眞愉快，林先生。我們將在下星期一以前，通知你本公司的最後決定。

應徵者：謝謝你，克拉克先生。再見。

面試者：再見。

2. Tour Guide

Tour Guides Needed Immediately

Are you absolutely fluent in English? Are you willing to work long hours? Do you like people? If you answered yes to all three questions, then call 2212-3136 for an interview.

面試者： Hello, Mr. Huang. Won't you sit down?
應徵者： Thank you.

面試者： I'm William Lewis. Nice to meet you.
應徵者： How do you do, Mr. Lewis? I'm glad to see you.

面試者： Now, you probably know that this interview is mostly to test your English, so just relax, and let's chat, shall we?
應徵者： All right.

面試者： Let's start with your identification. Please tell me your full name and present address.
應徵者： My name is Huang Kuo-hui, and my present address is 215 Heping East Road, Taipei.

2. 應徵導遊

急徵導遊

你的英語非常流利嗎？你願意長時間工作嗎？你喜歡人們嗎？如果你對上述三項問題的回答是肯定的話，請電2212-3136，約時間面試。

面試者：哈囉，黃先生。你不坐下來嗎？
應徵者：謝謝。

面試者：我是威廉・路易斯。很高興見到你。
應徵者：你好，路易斯先生。很高興和你見面。

面試者：現在，你可能知道，這次面試主要是測驗你的英語能力，所以放輕鬆點，我們聊聊好嗎？

應徵者：好的。

面試者：讓我們從你的身分開始。請告訴我，你的全名和現在的住址。
應徵者：我的名字是黃國輝，目前的住址是台北市和平東路215號。

面試者：How big is your family?

應徵者：There are four of us: my parents, a younger brother and I (me).

面試者：How do you get along with your brother?

應徵者：We get along very well. He's a junior at Taiwan University, majoring in economics. We go swimming and mountain climbing together a lot.

面試者：Do you think you are rather extroverted or introverted?

應徵者：Well, most of the time, I prefer being with a group of people, so I guess I am rather extroverted.

面試者：What college did you graduate from, and what subject did you major in?

應徵者：I graduated from Fu-jen University, and I majored in psychology.

面試者：One of the most important requirements for the job is the ability to speak English. Do you think you can use English to explain things to foreign tourists?

應徵者：Yes, I think I can. I've been attending an evening course in English conversation for two years, and I practice English conversation with my cassette tape recorder at home.

面試者：你們家有幾個人？

應徵者：我家有四個人，我的父母親、弟弟和我。

面試者：你和弟弟的相處情形如何？

應徵者：我們相處得很融洽。他是台灣大學三年級的學生，主修經濟學。我們常一起去游泳和登山。

面試者：你認爲自己是很外向還是很內向？

應徵者：嗯，大部分的時間，我比較喜歡和一群人在一起，所以我猜自己是相當外向的。

面試者：你是從哪所大學畢業的，主修什麼科目？

應徵者：我畢業於輔仁大學，我主修心理學。

面試者：英語會話能力是這項工作最重要的要求之一。你認爲你能用英語向外國觀光客解說嗎？

應徵者：是的，我想我可以。我在一家夜間英語會話班上了兩年的課，而且還會在家裡，配合著錄音帶練習英語會話。

面試者：Do you speak any other languages?

應徵者：I speak a little French and Japanese.

面試者：Why do you want to be a tour guide?

應徵者：I like to travel, and I also like meeting various kinds of people, so I think guiding foreign tourists would be very interesting. I want to show foreigners what a beautiful country this is.

面試者：Have you ever worked as a tour guide?

應徵者：I have a little experience. I guided a few foreign tourists around Taipei last year as a part-time job.

面試者：Do you have any licenses?

應徵者：Yes, I have guide license and driver's license.

面試者：Then you may know that it's hard work.

應徵者：Yes, I know. A friend of mine is a guide. He talked with me about his work, but I don't mind working hard.

面試者：Have you applied with any other companies?

應徵者：No, this is my first.

面試者：你會說其他別種語言嗎？

應徵者：我會說一點法語和日語。

面試者：你爲什麼想當導遊？

應徵者：我喜歡旅遊，而且我也喜歡認識各式各樣的人，所以，我認爲擔任外國觀光客的導遊會很有趣。我要讓外國人知道，這是個多麼美麗的國家。

面試者：你曾經當過導遊嗎？

應徵者：我有一點經驗。去年我帶領一些外國觀光客在台北觀光，那是兼差的工作。

面試者：你有任何執照嗎？

應徵者：是的，我有導遊執照和駕照。

面試者：那你可能已經知道，這是個辛苦的工作。

應徵者：是的，我知道。我有一個朋友是導遊，他跟我談過他的工作。但是我不介意工作辛苦。

面試者：你曾向其他公司應徵嗎？

應徵者：沒有，這是第一次。

面試者： Is there anything you want to ask about?

應徵者： I'd like to be an overseas tour guide someday. Would there ever be any chance of that?

面試者： Certainly. There'll be a good chance of that if you work for this company. Not right away, of course, but in a few years, after you learn more about our business, you may go overseas with a tour group. Any more questions?

應徵者： No, thank you. I found out most of the details of the working conditions and the salary during the Chinese language interview.

面試者： All right, then. We'll get in touch with you within a week. Thank you for coming today, Mr. Huang.

應徵者： Thank you. Good-bye.

面試者： Good-bye.

面試者： 你有其他任何事想問嗎？

應徵者： 我希望有一天能成爲海外導遊。我會有任何機會嗎？

面試者： 當然有。如果你在本公司工作，就會有這樣的好機會。當然不是馬上就有機會，但是幾年後，等你在本公司學到更多旅行實務，你就可以帶旅行團出國了。還有任何問題嗎？

應徵者： 沒有，謝謝。我在國語面談時，已經得知工作情況與薪水的細節了。

面試者： 好。我們會在一週內與你聯絡。謝謝你今天來面試，黃先生。

應徵者： 謝謝你，再見。

面試者： 再見。

3. English Secretary

English secretary wanted for foreign insurance company. Fluent spoken and written English, computer skills, strong communication and coordination skills required. 2524-7251, Miss Liu, M — F.

面試者： Come in, and take a seat, please.
應徵者： Thank you, Mr. Harris.

面試者： You are Chen Mei-yi, applying for the position of secretary?
應徵者： Yes, I am.

面試者： Well, let me tell you about this position. I need someone who takes dictation in English and transcribes it well.
應徵者： I see.

面試者： Do you think you speak English quite fluently? Tell me about your English education background.
應徵者： I must say my English is quite good. I got an excellent score on the TOFEL. And as you can see from my resume, I majored in English literature at college.

3. 應徵英文秘書

外國保險公司誠徵英文秘書。須英文説寫流利，會使用電腦，且溝通協調技巧出色。星期一至星期五電洽:2524-7251劉小姐。

面試者：請進，請坐。
應徵者：謝謝你，哈利斯先生。

面試者：妳是陳美宜，應徵秘書的職位？

應徵者：是，我是。

面試者：那麼，讓我告訴妳這個職位的相關事宜。我需要一個能夠聽寫英文，並且善加翻譯的人。

應徵者：我了解。

面試者：妳覺得妳的英語說得相當流利嗎？告訴我妳的英文教育背景。

應徵者：好的，我想我的英文相當好。我的托福成績很高。你可以從我的履歷表得知，我大學是主修英國文學的。

面試者：What computer software can you use?

應徵者：I can use MS-office, Word, Excel, and PowerPoint.

面試者：Your resume says that you worked in an insurance company for one year. What did you do there?

應徵者：I mainly set up schedules for my superior. Sometimes I answered phone calls from abroad.

面試者：May I ask why you left your last job, Miss Chen?

應徵者：I thought there wasn't any opportunity for advancement there. I decided to quit the job and take a computer course at a business institute in order to improve my office skills.

面試者：How was your attendance record at your previous job?

應徵者：I was seldom absent or late for work.

面試者：That's good. Are you familiar with the investment field?

應徵者：Well, I think I have general knowledge of investment. I learned about stocks and bonds at school. In addition, I like to read newspapers and financial magazines. I'd be willing to learn, however.

面試者：妳會使用哪些電腦軟體？

應徵者：我會用 MS-office, Word, Excel, 和 PowerPoint。

面試者：妳的履歷表上說，妳曾在保險公司待過一年，妳在那裡擔任什麼工作？

應徵者：我主要是幫我的上司排定行程，有時候接聽國外打來的電話。

面試者：陳小姐，我可以請問妳爲什麼辭掉原來的工作嗎？

應徵者：我想那裡沒有什麼升遷的機會。我決定辭掉那份工作，到商業學校再修點電腦課程，以增進我的工作能力。

面試者：妳在前一個工作的出勤記錄如何？

應徵者：我很少缺席或上班遲到。

面試者：很好。妳熟悉投資這個領域嗎？

應徵者：嗯，我想我有投資方面的常識。我在學校修過股票和債券的課。除此之外，我還喜歡看報紙和財經雜誌。不過，我很願意學習。

面試者： That's the important thing. By the way, are you married?

應徵者： No, I am not. I have no plans to marry in the near future. Do you encourage your female employees to quit after they get married?

面試者： We believe that is a personal decision. If a woman wishes to continue working for us after marrying, we are very glad to have her. Is there anything you would like to know about the job?

應徵者： Yes. What is your starting salary, and what sort of fringe benefits does the job offer?

面試者： The starting monthly salary would be 25,000 dollars, with raises after the first year according to your ability. There's a small bonus at the Lunar New Year, three weeks paid vacation a year, and health insurance.

應徵者： How about the working hours?

面試者： We work a five-day week, from nine to five, and there's rarely any overtime.

面試者： Well, how do you feel about the job, Miss Chen?

應徵者： I think it sounds like what I'm looking for.

面試者：那的確是很重要的。對了，妳結婚了嗎？

應徵者：不，還沒有。短期內也不打算結婚。你們希望貴公司的女性職員在結婚後離職嗎？

面試者：我們認爲那是依個人的決定。如果該名女性職員在結婚後，仍然希望爲我們工作的話，我們也樂於繼續雇用她。關於這份工作，妳還想知道些什麼？

應徵者：是的，你們起薪是多少？另外，這個工作提供哪些額外的福利？

面試者：起薪是每個月兩萬五千元，並在一年後，依照能力調薪。在農曆新年時，會有一些獎金，一年有三個星期的給薪假期，還有健保。

應徵者：工作的時間如何？

面試者：我們一星期工作五天，從九點到五點，很少加班。

面試者：嗯，陳小姐，妳對這個工作感覺如何？

應徵者：我覺得它聽起來像是我正想找的工作。

面試者： How can we contact you about our decision?

應徵者： You can call me at this number between four and six in the afternoon.

面試者： You'll be hearing from us within a few days. It's been pleasant talking with you. Thank you for coming.

應徵者： Thank you, Mr. Harris. Good-bye.

面試者： Good-bye.

面試者： 我如何通知妳本公司的決定呢？

應徵者： 你可以在下午四點到六點之間，打這個電話給我。

面試者： 妳會在幾天內接到我們的消息。很高興和妳談話，謝謝妳前來面試。

應徵者： 謝謝你，哈里斯先生。再見。

面試者： 再見。

4. Mechanical Engineer

The Turner Automotive Company needs a new, young engineer. Mr. Liu's former schoolmate at National Taiwan University, Mr. Chou, works for this company, and has advised Mr. Liu to apply for the position available. Mr. Liu has come for an interview with Mr. Brown.

面試者： Good morning. You're Mr. Liu?

應徵者： Yes, that's right.

面試者： Have a seat, please.

應徵者： Thank you, Mr. Brown.

面試者： Now, let me just check a few things. Your full name is Liu Hsin-hwa, right?

應徵者： Yes.

面試者： You graduated from National Taiwan University?

應徵者： Yes.

面試者： What did you major in?

應徵者： Mechanical engineering.

4. 應徵機械工程師

唐納汽車公司需要一位年輕的新工程師。劉先生在台大時的同學周先生，在該公司工作，他建議劉先生去應徵這個職位。劉先生前來和布朗先生面談。

面試者：早安，你是劉先生嗎？
應徵者：是的，沒錯。

面試者：請坐。
應徵者：謝謝你，布朗先生。

面試者：現在，讓我核對一下。你的全名是劉欣華，對嗎？

應徵者：是的。

面試者：你畢業於台灣大學嗎？

應徵者：是的。

面試者：你主修什麼？
應徵者：機械工程。

面試者：What is it that interests you about car manufacturing?

應徵者：There are lots of things, of course, but the most important one is the challenge, I think. I have loved cars since my childhood. I think cars are going to be more efficient than ever before, and the new materials make designs possible which no one imagined a few years ago.

面試者：Oh, you're primarily interested in design, then?

應徵者：Yes, designing cars is my first love, but if you hire me I'll do my best at any job you ask me to try.

面試者：What made you pick this company?

應徵者：Mr. Chou Chin-wen is from my university. He and I were in the electronics club together. He was a junior when I was a freshman, and we've kept in touch ever since then. He told me about his job here, and I became interested in this company. I think a five-day work week and nine-to-five working hours are a good system, and Mr. Chou also said that a person's advances in this company are based on his own merits, and not on his age or which university he graduated from.

面試者：你對汽車生產的哪一方面感興趣？

應徵者：當然，很多部分我都很有興趣，但是我想，最主要的，是有挑戰性。我從小就喜歡汽車。我認爲汽車的效能將比以往更高，而新的材料，會使幾年前無法想像的設計成爲可能。

面試者：哦，那麼你主要是對設計有興趣嗎？

應徵者：是的，設計汽車是我的最愛，但是如果您雇用我，我會盡力將您要求我嘗試的任何工作做好。

面試者：什麼原因使你選擇本公司？

應徵者：周志文先生和我來自同一所大學。他和我都參加了電子研究社。我大一時他大三，我們從那時起就一直保持聯絡。他告訴我有關他在這裡工作的情形，使我開始對貴公司感興趣。我認爲一星期工作五天，每天從九點上班到五點下班，是很好的工作制度。周先生還說，人事的升遷全看個人的表現，不管年紀或畢業的學校爲何。

面試者：Oh, yes, Mr. Chou told me you and he were friends. He recommended you quite highly, in fact. By the way, have you applied at any other company?

應徵者：Yes, I have applied at ABC Engineering Co., but that was just to get interview experience. It would be hard to develop my abilities in such a small company, I think. That's why I want to join this company.

面試者：Tell me what you know about our company.

應徵者：Well, this company is one of the biggest automobile makers in the world. The company was founded in New York in 1975 by James Turner, who is chairman. The president now is Benjamin Turner, his son.

面試者：Do you have any certificates?

應徵者：Yes, I got professional engineering license in the United States two years ago.

面試者：You may have chances to communicate with foreign engineers in our company. Can you deal with such situations?

應徵者：Of course I can. My TOEIC score was about 850. I believe I can deal with general situations, and communicate with foreign engineers in English.

面試者：喔，是的，周先生告訴我，你和他是朋友。事實上，他很推薦你。對了，你有應徵其他公司嗎？

應徵者：有的，我向 ABC 工程公司應徵過，但那只是爲了獲得面試經驗。我想在那麼小的公司很難發展我的能力，這也是我想進貴公司的理由。

面試者：告訴我，你對我們公司了解多少。

應徵者：嗯，貴公司是世界上最大的汽車製造公司之一。一九七五年由詹姆斯・唐納創立於紐約，他是當時的總裁。現在的總裁是他的兒子班哲明・唐納。

面試者：你有任何證照嗎？

應徵者：有，我兩年前在美國取得專業工程師執照。

面試者：在本公司，你可能會有機會要和外國工程師溝通。你能應付這種狀況嗎？

應徵者：我當然可以。我的多益測驗成績約爲 850 分。我相信我能用英語處理一般情況，並和外國工程師溝通。

面試者：What kind of things do you want from your future?

應徵者：I've wanted to be involved in engineering ever since I was little. If I pass this interview and am accepted into this company, I want to contribute to improving technology and making better cars. I want to be a professional in my field.

面試者：What kind of hobbies do you have?

應徵者：I like playing "go", a kind of oriental chess, and I also like mountaineering.

面試者：Is there anything you would like to know about the job?

應徵者：Yes. What is your starting salary, and what sort of fringe benefits does the job offer?

面試者：The starting salary for an engineer is 35,000 dollars a month, and raises would be given after the first six months according to your ability. There are semi-annual bonuses, three weeks paid vacation a year, and health insurance.

應徵者：One other question, if I may, sir.

面試者：Yes?

應徵者：Will there be any chance I might work abroad in the future?

面試者：你希望在未來得到什麼？

應徵者：從小我就希望與工程爲伍，如果我通過面試，並且進入貴公司，我將爲提升技術和製造更好的機器貢獻心力。我要成爲我這個領域內的專家。

面試者：你有什麼嗜好？

應徵者：我喜歡下「圍棋」，是一種東方棋，我也喜歡爬山。

面試者：關於這份工作，你還有什麼想知道的？

應徵者：有的。起薪是多少，以及這份工作提供什麼特別的福利嗎？

面試者：工程師的起薪是每個月三萬五千元，六個月後依能力調薪。每半年有獎金，每年有三個星期的給薪假期，和健保。

應徵者：先生，如果可以的話，我想再請教一個問題。

面試者：什麼？

應徵者：我以後有到國外工作的機會嗎？

面試者：Yes, after three years there will be a chance that you might be transferred overseas.

應徵者：That'd be good.

面試者：Well, Mr. Liu. I've enjoyed talking with you, but I have another appointment in just a few minutes. Thank you very much for coming today.

應徵者：Thank you, Mr. Brown.

面試者：You'll be hearing a definite answer from us within a week. Good-bye.

應徵者：Good-bye.

面試者：有，三年後你可能會有機會調到國外工作。

應徵者：那很好。

面試者：嗯，劉先生，很高興和你談話，但是我再過幾分鐘後還有約會。非常謝謝你今天來面試。

應徵者：謝謝您，布朗先生。

面試者：我們會在一星期內給你明確的答覆。再見。

應徵者：再見。

5. Bank Officer

Bank officer wanted by the First Bank. Experience necessary. Apply in person at 151 Cingdao East Road, 1-5 p.m., before 6 / 25.

面試者： May I help you?

應徵者： Yes, I'm here to apply for the position of bank officer.

面試者： I'm Mary Kelly. May I ask your name?

應徵者： My name is Chuang Ling-yu. How do you do, Miss Kelly?

面試者： I'm glad to meet you, Miss Chuang. Sit down, please.

應徵者： Thank you, Miss Kelly.

面試者： What are your qualifications for being a bank officer?

應徵者： I have been employed by Macoto Bank for three years, and I have two business management licenses. Furthermore, I'm experienced in investment planning.

5. 應徵銀行辦事員

第一銀行誠徵辦事員。需經驗。請在六月二十五日以前，每天下午一點至五點，至青島東路151號面洽。

面試者：我能幫什麼忙嗎？
應徵者：是的，我來應徵銀行辦事員的職位。

面試者：我是瑪麗・凱利。請問妳叫什麼名字？
應徵者：我叫做莊玲玉，妳好，凱利小姐。

面試者：很高興見到妳，莊小姐，請坐。

應徵者：謝謝妳，凱利小姐。

面試者：請問妳具備什麼樣的資格，來擔任銀行辦事員呢？
應徵者：我在誠泰銀行服務了三年，且擁有兩張商業管理執照。此外，我對投資規劃很有經驗。

面試者： Would you be willing to take a test?

應徵者： Yes, I would.

(*after testing*)

面試者： Your financial concepts and knowledge are pretty good. The interviewer, Mr. McBride, is waiting for you. Let's go to his office.

(*In Mr. McBride's office.*)

面試者： Won't you sit down, Miss Chuang?

應徵者： Thank you, Mr. McBride.

面試者： Can you tell me about your education?

應徵者： Well, I graduated from First Girls' High School, and then studied at National Taiwan University. I majored in Finance and minored in Information Management.

面試者： Can you speak English fluently? Sometimes we may have foreign customers.

應徵者： I think I can introduce and explain any kind of investment project in English.

面試者： Very good. Have you had any sales experience?

應徵者： A little. When I was in college, I had a part-time job in my father's office.

面試者：妳願意接受測驗嗎？

應徵者：是的，我願意。

（測驗後）

面試者：妳的財務觀念和知識都很出色。面試官麥克布萊德先生正在等妳。我們去他的辦公室吧。

（在麥克．布萊德先生的辦公室裡）

面試者：請坐吧，莊小姐？

應徵者：謝謝你，麥克布萊德先生。

面試者：能告訴我妳的教育背景嗎？

應徵者：嗯，我畢業於北一女中，然後進入國立台灣大學就讀。我主修財務金融，輔修資訊管理。

面試者：妳英文說得流利嗎？有時我們可能會碰到外國客戶。

應徵者：我想我能用英語介紹和解釋任何一種投資計畫。

面試者：很好。妳有任何業務經驗嗎？

應徵者：一點點。我唸大學時，曾在父親的公司打工。

面試者：What did you do there?

應徵者：I'm afraid I did only simple jobs, such as answering the telephone and introducing new products to our customers.

面試者：Did you use English there?

應徵者：Not very often, but sometimes someone would call and speak in English on the phone. Once in a while I even greeted foreign visitors in English.

面試者：Do you like to work with figures?

應徵者：Yes, I like math. And I'm sure I'm a discreet person.

面試者：Your job here would include investment planning. You would have to visit our customers personally.

應徵者：That's OK. I think I'll enjoy my work. By the way, what would my hours be?

面試者：Your hours would be from nine to five with an hour for lunch. We also have two coffee breaks.

應徵者：What about the salary?

面試者：You would be paid NT$26,000 on probation and after three months you'd get a raise if your work were satisfactory.

面試者：妳在那裡做些什麼？

應徵者：恐怕我只是做些簡單的工作，像接電話和向客戶介紹新產品。

面試者：妳在那裡使用英文嗎？

應徵者：不常，但有時候電話裡會有人說英語，我甚至偶爾用英語接待外國訪客。

面試者：妳喜歡做與數字有關的工作嗎？

應徵者：是的，我喜歡數學。而且我確信我是個謹慎的人。

面試者：妳在這裡的工作，將包含投資規劃。妳可能還必須親自拜訪客戶。

應徵者：沒問題，我想我會喜歡我的工作。對了，我必須工作幾個小時？

面試者：妳的工作時間是從九點到五點，有一小時的午餐時間。我們還有兩次短暫的休息時間。

應徵者：待遇如何？

面試者：試用期是每個月兩萬六千元，三個月之後，如果工作表現令人滿意，就會加薪。

應徵者： Do you have any fringe benefits?

面試者： We offer a Christmas bonus, a two-week vacation each year, and free health insurance, and you would be entitled to 16‰ annual interest on your savings account in our bank.

應徵者： That sounds good.

面試者： What do you consider important when looking for a job, Miss Chuang?

應徵者： I think the most important thing is doing interesting work. Pleasant working conditions with a cooperative staff are also important to me. I want a job in which I can respect the people I work with.

面試者： I appreciate that. We're looking for a dependable and well-qualified person.

應徵者： May I ask if there would be any Saturday work?

面試者： No, we don't work on Saturdays. By the way, where do you live, Miss Chuang?

應徵者： I live in Sindian. It takes about half an hour to get here by bus.

面試者： Do you live with your family?

應徵者： Yes. I live with my parents and brother.

面試者： I see. You know we put much importance on regular attendance and punctuality.

應徵者：有沒有什麼特別的福利？
面試者：我們有聖誕節獎金，每年有兩星期的假，以及免費的健康保險，同時，妳的存款可以享有千分之十六的年利率。

應徵者：聽起來不錯。

面試者：莊小姐，當妳找工作時，妳認爲什麼最重要？

應徵者：我想最重要的，就是要做有趣的工作。愉快的工作環境和合作的同事，對我來說也很重要。我想找一個我能尊敬所有同事的工作。

面試者：我欣賞妳的看法。我們正在找一個值得信賴、而且有能力的人。

應徵者：請問星期六要上班嗎？
面試者：不，我們星期六不上班。對了，妳住在哪裡，莊小姐？

應徵者：我住在新店，搭公車到這裡大概半小時。

面試者：妳和家人住在一起嗎？
應徵者：是的，我和我爸媽還有弟弟住在一起。

面試者：我明白了。妳知道我們很重視出席率和準時上班的。

面試者：We would very much like to consider you for the position. If we hire you, when would you be able to start work?

應徵者：I can start anytime.

面試者：We'll call you as soon as we have made our decision. What is your number?

應徵者：My number is 2707-1413

面試者：Thank you for coming today.

應徵者：It was my pleasure. Thank you, Mr. McBride

面試者：Not at all.

面試者：我們很樂意考慮由妳來擔任這項職務。如果我們錄用妳，妳什麼時候可以開始上班？

應徵者：任何時間都可以。

面試者：我們一決定就會打電話通知妳。妳的電話號碼是多少？

應徵者：我的電話號碼是 2707-1413。

面試者：謝謝妳今天來面試。

應徵者：這是我的榮幸。謝謝您，麥克布萊德先生。

面試者：不客氣。

6. Customer Service Personnel

ABC International ran an ad in the China News. It read as follows:

> Large international corporation seeks English-speaking customer service personnel. Fluency in English a must, service industry experience preferred. Good salary, benefits. 2319-6624, Personnel Department.

Miss Lee is a receptionist at an American company. She wants to apply for the job, so she dials the number.

總　機：ABC International. May I help you?

應徵者：Please give me the Personnel Department.

面試者：Personnel Department, Mr. Cornell speaking.

應徵者：Good morning. I am calling in answer to your advertisement in the newspaper for English-speaking customer service personnel.

面試者：Oh, I see. May I have your name, please?

應徵者：This is Lee Pao-ling speaking.

面試者：Please tell me about your education and work experience.

應徵者：I graduated from Hsingwu College and have been working for an American company for two years.

6. 應徵客服人員

ABC 國際公司在中華日報刊登了一則廣告，其內容如下：

大型國際公司誠徵英語客服人員。須英文流利，有服務業經驗者佳，高薪、福利佳，電洽 2319-6624 人事部。

李小姐是一家美國公司的接待員，她想應徵這份工作，所以撥了這個號碼。

總　機：ABC 國際公司。我能幫您什麼嗎？
應徵者：請幫我轉人事部。

面試者：人事部，我是康奈爾先生。
應徵者：早安，我打電話來，是想要應徵貴公司登報徵求的英語客服人員一職。

面試者：哦，我明白了，請問妳叫什麼名字。
應徵者：我叫李寶玲。

面試者：請告訴我妳的學歷和工作經驗。

應徵者：我畢業於醒吾技術學院，已在一家美國公司工作兩年。

面試者：What did you major in at college?

應徵者：I majored in International Trade.

面試者：Did you learn English conversation from a native speaker?

應徵者：Yes, I have been attending an English conversation class at a private institute for two years, where Americans teach.

面試者：What kind of job do you have at the American company?

應徵者：I am a receptionist.

面試者：Have you had any experience on the switchboard?

應徵者：Yes, sometimes I relieve the girl on the switchboard when she takes a break.

面試者：You speak English pretty well. Would you like to come here for an interview?

應徵者：I certainly would.

面試者：How about Wednesday at two o'clock?

應徵者：That'll be fine.

面試者：妳在技術學院裡主修什麼科目？

應徵者：我主修國際貿易。

面試者：妳曾向以英語爲母語的人學過英語會話嗎？

應徵者：是的，我已在一個由美國老師任教的私立機構，上了兩年的英語會話課。

面試者：妳在那家美國公司擔任什麼工作？

應徵者：我是接待員。

面試者：妳有當總機的經驗嗎？

應徵者：是的，有時總機小姐休息時，我去幫她的忙。

面試者：妳英語說得非常好。妳願意來面談嗎？

應徵者：我當然願意。

面試者：星期三下午兩點好嗎？

應徵者：好。

面試者：Please bring your resume and come to room 707 in the World Building. Ask for Mr. Cornell.

應徵者：Room 707 in the World Building, Mr. Cornell?

面試者：That's right. I look forward to seeing you then.

應徵者：I'm looking forward to it, too. Thank you.

面試者：Thank you for calling. Good-bye.

應徵者：Good-bye.

(*2:00 p.m. on Wednesday, at Mr. Cornell's office*)

面試者：Ah, Miss Lee! Sit down, please. Which do you like, coffee or tea?

應徵者：Oh, thank you. Coffee, please. Here is my resume.

面試者：Can you speak any foreign language other than English?

應徵者：I studied a little French at college.

面試者：I see. You would be using mainly English on this job. Do you think you can manage English telephone conversations?

應徵者：Yes, I think I can in ordinary circumstances.

面試者：請帶履歷表到世界大樓 707 室，找康奈爾先生。

應徵者：世界大樓 707 室，康奈爾先生，是嗎？

面試者：沒錯。希望到時候能見到妳。

應徵者：我也希望如此。謝謝你。

面試者：謝謝妳打電話來。再見。

應徵者：再見。

（星期三下午兩點，在康奈爾先生的辦公室）

面試者：啊，李小姐！請坐。妳要咖啡還是茶？

應徵者：哦，謝謝，請給我咖啡。這是我的履歷表。

面試者：妳會說英語以外的其他外語嗎？

應徵者：我在技術學院學過一些法文。

面試者：我明白了。這份工作主要是使用英文。妳想妳能應付電話的英語會話嗎？

應徵者：是的，我想一般的情形，我都能應付。

面試者：Would you be able to do shift work? Sometimes you would have to work the night shift.

應徵者：No problem. May I ask the starting salary?

面試者：We pay twenty-three thousand dollars monthly to start. It's our policy to hire on a trial basis. If you work out all right, after three months you'll be put on the permanent payroll and be given a raise. We give bonuses semi-annually.

應徵者：How about the vacations?

面試者：Our girls have a two-week summer vacation. Do you have any other questions?

應徵者：No, I think that's all.

面試者：Well, what do you think? Are you interested in the job?

應徵者：Yes, I am.

面試者：Well, then, Miss Lee, we'll get in touch with you within a week. Shall we notify you of our decision by mail, or by telephone?

應徵者：By telephone, please. Do you have my number?

面試者：Yes, I see it is here on the resume. Thank you very much for coming, Miss Lee.

應徵者：It's been nice talking with you, Mr. Cornell. Thank you very much. Good-bye.

面試者：Good-bye.

面試者：妳能配合輪班嗎？妳有時候可能必須值夜班。

應徵者：沒問題。我可以知道起薪是多少嗎？

面試者：我們的起薪是每個月兩萬三千元，這是公司規定，試用期間的薪水。如果工作情況良好，三個月後，妳就能升為正職，而且會加薪。我們每半年發一次獎金。

應徵者：那休假方面呢？

面試者：本公司的女性職員，在夏天有兩星期的假期。妳還有其他問題嗎？

應徵者：不，我想沒有了。

面試者：那麼，妳覺得怎麼樣？妳對這份工作有興趣嗎？

應徵者：是的。

面試者：那麼，李小姐，我們會在一星期內和妳聯絡。我們應該用信件，還是用電話通知妳我們的決定？

應徵者：請用電話通知我。你知道我的電話號碼嗎？

面試者：是的，我看到履歷表上有。非常感謝妳今天來面談，李小姐。

應徵者：很高興和你談話，康奈爾先生。非常感謝你。再見。

面試者：再見。

7. Flight Attendant

Trans Global Airways is now accepting applications for the position of flight attendant. Applicants must speak English and like to travel around the world. Send resume to P.O. Box 17-191, Taipei.

面試者： Take a seat, please, Miss Huang.
應徵者： Thank you, Mr. Smith.

面試者： Thank you for your interest in this position. Why do you consider yourself qualified for this kind of work?
應徵者： I like to meet various kinds of people, and I think I speak fairly good English.

面試者： I know from your resume that you are working as an office girl in a Chinese company. Why do you plan to change jobs?
應徵者： I would like to have a job that is more lively than my present one, and I would like to speak English in my work.

面試者： Have you ever traveled abroad?
應徵者： Yes, I traveled to Europe two years ago after I graduated from junior college. I love to travel.

7. 應徵空服員

環球航空公司正在招考空服員。應徵者必須會說英語，並且喜歡到世界各地旅行。履歷表請寄到台北郵政 17-191 號信箱。

面試者：請坐，黃小姐。
應徵者：謝謝你，史密斯先生。

面試者：謝謝妳對這個職務感興趣。妳爲什麼覺得自己適合這份工作呢？

應徵者：我喜歡和各種不同的人接觸，而且我認爲我的英語說得相當好。

面試者：從妳的履歷，我知道妳正在一家中國的公司上班。妳爲什麼打算換工作？

應徵者：我想找一個比目前更活潑的工作，而且我希望能在工作時說英語。

面試者：妳曾經到國外旅行嗎？
應徵者：是的，我兩年前從二專畢業之後，曾到歐洲旅行。我喜歡旅行。

面試者：I see. By the way, have you ever had any serious illness?

應徵者：No, I have always been in good health.

面試者：This type of work requires a great deal of stamina. You'd be on your feet most of the time and sometimes you would be expected to work long hours. Flight attendants have to be in top physical condition. Are you familiar with the duties of a flight attendant?

應徵者：Yes, some of my friends are flight attendants, and I've heard about their duties.

面試者：Do you know what should a terrific flight attendant be?

應徵者：I think he or she should be thoughtful, helpful, and professional.

面試者：What will you do if you can't communicate with your passenger?

應徵者：First, I will try to use hand gestures or body language. If my passenger still doesn't know what I mean, I will ask my co-workers to help me out.

面試者：When would you be available to start working?

應徵者：Well, I would have to give at least a month's notice at my present job, so I could probably report for work by the first of November.

面試者：我明白了。對了，妳曾經生過重病嗎？

應徵者：不，我的健康狀況一直很好。

面試者：這種工作需要大量的體力。大多數的時間，妳都必須站著，而且有時候妳會被要求長時間工作。空服員必須要有極佳的健康狀況。妳熟悉空服員的職務嗎？

應徵者：是的，我有一些朋友是空服員，所以我聽說過她們的職務。

面試者：妳知道一位出色的空服員應該是怎麼樣的嗎？

應徵者：我想他（她）應該是體貼、樂於助人，而且很專業。

面試者：如果妳無法和乘客溝通時，妳會怎麼做？

應徵者：首先，我會試著使用手勢或肢體語言。如果乘客仍然無法了解我的意思，我會請同事來協助我。

面試者：妳什麼時候可以開始工作？

應徵者：嗯，我目前的工作至少必須在一個月前提出辭呈，所以我大概可以在十一月一日來報到。

面試者： Our next training program begins on November 12th. Do you have any questions you'd like to ask me, Miss Huang?

應徵者： Would there be opportunities to work abroad in the future?

面試者： Yes, there's a good chance you'd be transferred after two years to a foreign airport. Would that be satisfactory to you?

應徵者： I'd like that very much.

面試者： As you may know, we pay our flight attendants 25,000 dollars monthly to start. Raises are given according to your ability. You'd receive such fringe benefits as bonus pay, travel and hotel discounts, health insurance, and a month's vacation each year.

應徵者： May I ask how much bonuses are?

面試者： Certainly. We offer semi-annual bonuses equivalent to three month's salary at the present time. Of course, the amount of the bonus is flexible.

應徵者： I understand that.

面試者： Well, what do you think? Are you still interested in the job?

應徵者： Yes, I am.

面試者：我們下一次的訓練課程是從十一月十二日開始。妳有任何問題想問我嗎，黃小姐？

應徵者：請問將來有沒有到國外工作的機會？

面試者：有，兩年後會有個好機會，妳可能被調往國外的機場。這樣妳滿意嗎？

應徵者：我非常滿意。

面試者：正如妳所知，本公司的空服員起薪是每個月兩萬五千元，再依能力調薪。妳可以享有一些特別的福利，例如：獎金、旅行，和旅館的折扣、健康保險，以及每年一個月的休假。

應徵者：我可以知道獎金有多少嗎？

面試者：當然可以。目前我們半年的獎金相當於三個月的薪水。當然，獎金的金額大小是有彈性的。

應徵者：我知道。

面試者：那麼，妳覺得如何？妳仍然對這份工作有興趣嗎？

應徵者：是的。

面試者：You can feel assured that we will give your application careful consideration. We'll let you know our decision as soon as possible. How can we get in touch with you?

應徵者：I can be reached at my home in the evenings. My telephone number is 2707-1413.

面試者：That's 2707-1413?

應徵者：That's right.

面試者：You'll be hearing from us within ten days. Thank you for coming, Miss Huang.

應徵者：Thank you, Mr. Smith. Good-bye.

面試者：Good-bye.

面試者：妳可以放心，我們將會仔細考慮妳的應徵，同時也會儘快讓妳知道我們的決定。我們要如何與妳聯絡？

應徵者：晚上可以在我家聯絡到我。我的電話號碼是 2707-1413。

面試者：是 2707-1413 嗎？

應徵者：對。

面試者：妳將在十天之內接到我們的消息。謝謝妳今天前來面試，黃小姐。

應徵者：謝謝你，史密斯先生。再見。

面試者：再見。

8. Marketing Planner

Mr. Ho knew of an opening in the Marketing Division of the company for which he works, and told his friend Mr. Yang about it. Mr. Yang, who has worked at a bank for two years, has arranged an interview with Mr. Ford, the manager of this company's Marketing Division.

面試者： Good afternoon. You are Mr. Yang Ching-li?

應徵者： That's right.

面試者： Please make yourself comfortable. Smoke if you like.

應徵者： Thank you, Mr. Ford.

面試者： Tell me about your education, please.

應徵者： I graduated from Tamkang University two years ago. I majored in business administration.

面試者： Your resume says that you've been working at an American bank for the last two years.

應徵者： Yes, that's right.

8. 應徵行銷企劃員

何先生得知在他服務的公司，有一個行銷部門的空缺，所以就告訴他的朋友楊先生。楊先生在一家銀行工作了兩年，他和該公司的銷售部經理福特先生，約定了一次面談。

面試者：午安。你是楊慶立先生嗎？
應徵者：是的。

面試者：請不要拘束。你可以吸煙，如果你想的話。

應徵者：謝謝你，福特先生。

面試者：請告訴我你的教育背景。
應徵者：我兩年前從淡江大學畢業，主修企業管理。

面試者：你在履歷表上說，過去兩年，你都在一家美國銀行工作。
應徵者：是的，沒錯。

面試者： Why do you want to change jobs?

應徵者： (*smile*) I'm sure you are familiar with banking systems in Taiwan, Mr. Ford. The jobs given to young men are not very challenging, and I didn't graduate from a famous university, so my chances of going very far in the bank are not very good. Mr. Ho Li-min and I are old friends from school and went out one night and got to talking. I told him I didn't like the job I had, and he said there were sometimes openings at the company where he was working.

面試者： When was this?

應徵者： Six months ago. I went home and thought about it. And then I started doing some research into your company. I liked what I found out, so when Mr. Ho called me up last month and said there was an opening in marketing, I sent my resume in.

面試者： What did you see that you liked so much?

應徵者： Your Taipei office opened only two years ago, and you are just starting to grow. It looks to me as if there will be a lot of challenging work and a chance for me to advance according to my ability.

面試者： And what do you think you would bring to the job?

應徵者： My banking experience, mostly. I know a lot about how the Taiwan economy works, and how business is done in this country. And I'm a hard worker when I have something challenging to do.

面試者：你爲什麼想換工作？

應徵者：（微笑）我相信您對台灣的銀行體系很熟悉，福特先生。那種工作對年輕人沒有什麼挑戰性，而且我不是從名校畢業，所以我在銀行的升遷機會不是很好。何立民先生和我，從在學校時就是老朋友，有天晚上一起出去聊天。我告訴他，我不喜歡我的工作，他說他服務的公司，有時會有空缺。

面試者：這是什麼時候的事？

應徵者：六個月前。我回家之後考慮了一下，然後開始對貴公司作一些研究。我很喜歡我的發現，所以當何先生上個月打電話告訴我，行銷部門有空缺時，我就寄履歷表來了。

面試者：你看到本公司的哪一方面，是你很喜歡的？

應徵者：你們的台北公司兩年前才開業，而且目前正在成長中。對我而言，似乎有許多富有挑戰性的工作，和依照能力升遷的機會。

面試者：你認爲你能爲這份工作帶來什麼？

應徵者：大部分是我在銀行的經驗。我很了解台灣經濟運作的情形，和國內做生意的方式。當有具挑戰性的工作可做時，我工作時會非常勤奮。

面試者：I think employees here have to have a good command of English. How about your ability to speak and understand English?

應徵者：I have been attending an evening course in English conversation for three years, so I think I speak English fairly well. And I read books and magazines in English regularly.

面試者：What computer software are you acquainted with?

應徵者：I'm acquainted with MS-Office, Word, Excel, and PowerPoint.

面試者：What are your hobbies?

應徵者：I like sports, especially swimming and playing tennis. And I also like listening to classical music.

面試者：Tell me about your family.

應徵者：There are my mother and younger sister. My father died long ago, so I support my family. My sister is a college student.

面試者：I see. Are you familiar with our pay scale? We'd expect you to start a little lower than what you are earning at the bank now, but you would be eligible for a raise after the first six months. We offer full insurance, two weeks paid vacation and a five-day work week, but we do expect you to do overtime when it's necessary. Is that acceptable?

應徵者：Yes, that's fine.

面試者：我想我們這裡的職員英文必須很好。你的英文聽講能力如何？

應徵者：我已經參加了三年的英語會話夜間課程，所以我想我的英文說得很好。而且我還會定期閱讀英文書籍和雜誌。

面試者：你熟悉哪些電腦軟體？

應徵者：我熟悉 MS-Office, Word, Excel, 和 PowerPoint。

面試者：你的嗜好是什麼？

應徵者：我喜歡運動，特別是游泳和打網球。我還喜歡聽古典音樂。

面試者：談談你的家庭。

應徵者：我家裡有母親和一個妹妹。我父親很早以前就去世，所以由我負擔家計。我妹妹是大學生。

面試者：我知道了。你清楚我們的薪資級別嗎？我們預期在一開始時，你賺得會比現在待在銀行少，但是六個月以後，將有資格調薪。我們提供全險和兩星期的給薪假期，一星期工作五天，但我們希望必要時你能加班。這樣你能接受嗎？

應徵者：是的，可以。

面試者：One more thing. Would you be willing to work overseas if the office asked you to?

應徵者：Yes, of course.

面試者：All right. We'll let you know our final decision within five days. Thank you for coming.

應徵者：Thank you. I look forward to hearing from you. Good-bye.

面試者：Good-bye.

面試者： 還有一件事。如果公司要求你到國外工作，你會願意嗎？

應徵者： 是的，當然。

面試者： 好的。我們會在五天內，讓你知道我們的最後決定。謝謝你來面試。

應徵者： 謝謝。我很期待接到你的回覆。再見。

面試者： 再見。

面試考題一覽表

<table>
<tr><th>基　本　必　考　題</th><th>進　階　必　考　題</th></tr>
<tr><td>請簡短的介紹一下自己。</td><td>談談你對本公司的了解。</td></tr>
<tr><td>你的興趣是什麼？</td><td>你了解自己所應徵的職務嗎？</td></tr>
<tr><td>你的個性如何？外向還是內向？</td><td>你覺得自己具備什麼應徵資格？</td></tr>
<tr><td>你有哪些優缺點？</td><td>假如工作碰到障礙，你會如何處理？</td></tr>
<tr><td>你有什麼特殊技能嗎？</td><td>你最喜歡或討厭和怎樣的人共事？</td></tr>
<tr><td>你擅長哪些語言？</td><td>你爲什麼辭掉上一份工作？</td></tr>
<tr><td>你有任何證照或執照嗎？</td><td>你最崇拜的成功人物是誰？</td></tr>
<tr><td>談談你的家庭狀況。</td><td>你最近是否有報名參加進修課程？</td></tr>
<tr><td>談談你的求學過程。</td><td>你還有繼續深造的打算嗎？</td></tr>
<tr><td>大學是唸什麼科系？</td><td rowspan="2">如果工作經常需要加班或出差，你能接受嗎？</td></tr>
<tr><td>爲什麼選擇唸這個科系？</td></tr>
<tr><td>有參加過社團嗎？</td><td rowspan="2">若公司要求轉調大陸分公司，你會願意配合嗎？</td></tr>
<tr><td>是否有打工經驗？</td></tr>
<tr><td>爲什麼來應徵這份工作？</td><td rowspan="2">你如何紓解工作壓力，或克服工作低潮期？</td></tr>
<tr><td>你對未來兩年有什麼計劃？</td></tr>
<tr><td>談談過去的工作經驗。</td><td rowspan="2">除了應徵本公司之外，你是否也應徵其他公司？</td></tr>
<tr><td>你希望的待遇爲何？</td></tr>
<tr><td>你願意配合加班嗎？</td><td>如果本公司錄取你，你認爲你會在本公司服務幾年？</td></tr>
<tr><td>你何時可以來上班？</td><td>你覺得要成爲一個成功的辦事員（應徵職位），需要具備哪些特質與能力？</td></tr>
</table>

挑　戰　題	主　動　出　擊　題
請用英文自我介紹。	可否請您描述一下貴公司的部門組織？
你找工作最在意什麼條件？	可否請您描述一下貴公司的業務範圍？
你認爲自己有哪些方面需要加強？	您心目中的理想人選，須具備何種經歷或特質？
如果你是本公司的面試官，你會錄用你自己嗎？	進入貴公司是否需要某些商業證照或科技執照？
談談你最近讀的一本書或雜誌。	若我有機會於貴公司服務，我該如何配合未來的主管？
這幾天最吸引你的新聞議題是什麼？	
你對 SARS 事件有何想法？	貴公司是否有培訓新人的課程？
你有沒有哪些方面優於其他應徵者？	貴公司是否提供在職進修的課程？

行政院青年輔導委員會
九十三年第四季青年創業輔導申辦說明會日程表

地　區	日　期	地　點
北區(一)	10 / 02 (六) 11 / 06 (六) 12 / 04 (六)	台北市和平東路一段129-1號 師大綜合大樓202演講廳
北區(二)	10 / 23 (六) 11 / 20 (六) 12 / 18 (六)	板橋市府中路29之1號14樓 第十會議室
桃園區	10 / 23 (六) 11 / 27 (六) 12 / 18 (六)	桃園市縣府路59號 桃園縣勞工育樂中心
台中區	10 / 16 (六) 11 / 20 (六) 12 / 18 (六)	台中市天保街60號 世貿中心2樓工研院台中工服部
台南區	10 / 09 (六) 11 / 13 (六) 12 / 11 (六)	台南市中華西路2段34號 台南市社教館2樓會議室
高雄區	10 / 16 (六) 11 / 20 (六) 12 / 18 (六)	高雄市三民區九如一路720號地下1樓 科學工藝博物館 慈香庭演講廳

備註： 1. 說明會課程內容包括「創業貸款法規與青年創業計劃書填寫說明」,「向銀行辦理青創貸款應注意事項」，對申請青創貸款有極大的幫助，使欲創業者在創業的起步上「快、易、通」。

2. 以上說明會時間皆爲下午一時三十分至四時。

3. 申請人可在各區說明會辦理時間內，現場報名免費參加。

4. 洽詢電話：(02) 2322-3006

網址：www.nyc.gov.tw/part1/a14.htm

4. More Information

補充資料

1 求職注意事項

1. 如何提高履歷表的被閱讀率

(1) 排版不要過於緊密或鬆散。一般而言，字間以固定行高 22pt 最佳，中文斷句不空格，英文斷句空兩格。段與段之間至少要空一行的距離。

(2) 善用字體變化強調重點，對於被履歷表淹沒的雇主來說，具有一目了然的功效。

(3) 裝訂完整，一般而言是裝訂在左上角，不妨使用色彩亮麗的迴紋針略加裝飾，可以增加履歷被抽出來閱讀的可能性。

(4) 一個段落不可過於冗長，若內容較多，可以考慮用分項條列的方式呈現。

2. 面試必備用品

(1) 履歷表	(8) 手錶
(2) 一吋及兩吋照片各兩張	(9) 大小合宜的提袋
(3) 身分證	(10) 面試通知單
(4) 筆記本、備忘錄	(11) 應徵公司簡介資料
(5) 文具用品	(12) 相關證書文件
(6) 地圖、應徵公司地址、聯絡電話	(13) 梳子、鏡子
(7) 手帕及面紙	

2 建議使用字彙

無論是撰寫履歷表，或是面對面的口試，善用積極正面的字彙來描述自己的特質和個性，將有助於面試官給予較高的評價。以下為建議多加使用的字彙：

active〔ˈæktɪv〕*adj.* 積極的

adaptive〔əˈdæptɪv〕*adj.* 適應的

affable〔ˈæfəbl̩〕
adj. 和藹可親的；友善的

alert〔əˈlɝt〕
adj. 機警的；敏捷的

amiable〔ˈemɪəbl̩〕
adj. 和藹可親的；厚道的

apt〔æpt〕*adj.* 聰明的

attentive〔əˈtɛntɪv〕
adj. 體貼的；殷勤的

brave〔brev〕*adj.* 勇敢的

capable〔ˈkepəbl̩〕*adj.* 能幹的

cautious〔ˈkɔʃəs〕*adj.* 謹慎的

cheerful〔ˈtʃɪrfəl〕
adj. 樂意的；有誠意的

clear-headed〔ˈklɪrˈhɛdɪd〕
adj. 頭腦清楚的

clever〔ˈklɛvɚ〕*adj.* 聰明的

competent〔ˈkɑmpətənt〕
adj. 能幹的

confident〔ˈkɑnfədənt〕
adj. 有自信的

conscientious〔ˌkɑnʃɪˈɛnʃəs〕
adj. 正直的；負責盡職的

considerate〔kənˈsɪdərɪt〕
adj. 體貼的

cool-headed〔ˈkulˈhɛdɪd〕
adj. 頭腦冷靜的

courageous〔kəˈredʒəs〕
adj. 勇敢的

courteous〔ˈkɝtɪəs〕
adj. 有禮貌的

dependable〔dɪˈpɛndəbl̩〕
adj. 可信賴的

diligent〔ˈdɪlədʒənt〕*adj.* 勤勉的

diplomatic〔ˌdɪpləˈmætɪk〕
adj. 圓滑的；有交際手腕的

earnest〔ˈɜnɪst〕*adj.* 熱心的
efficient〔əˈfɪʃənt〕*adj.* 有效率的
elastic〔ɪˈlæstɪk〕*adj.* 適應力強的
energetic〔ˌɛnəˈdʒɛtɪk〕*adj.* 充滿活力的
enterprising〔ˈɛntəˌpraɪzɪŋ〕*adj.* 有進取心的
extrovert〔ˈɛkstroˌvɜt〕*adj.* 外向的
friendly〔ˈfrɛndlɪ〕*adj.* 友善的
generous〔ˈdʒɛnərəs〕*adj.* 慷慨的
gracious〔ˈgreʃəs〕*adj.* 優雅的
gregarious〔grɪˈgɛrɪəs〕*adj.* 合群的；愛交朋友的
happy-go-lucky〔ˈhæpɪˌgoˈlʌkɪ〕*adj.* 樂天的
healthy〔ˈhɛlθɪ〕*adj.* 健康的
helpful〔ˈhɛlpfəl〕*adj.* 肯幫忙的
honest〔ˈɑnɪst〕*adj.* 誠實的
humorous〔ˈhjumərəs〕*adj.* 幽默的
independent〔ˌɪndɪˈpɛndənt〕*adj.* 獨立的
industrious〔ɪnˈdʌstrɪəs〕*adj.* 勤勉的
intelligent〔ɪnˈtɛlədʒənt〕*adj.* 聰明的
lively〔ˈlaɪvlɪ〕*adj.* 活潑的
loyal〔ˈlɔɪəl〕*adj.* 忠實的
openhearted〔ˈopənˈhɑrtɪd〕*adj.* 坦白的
open-minded〔ˈopənˈmaɪndɪd〕*adj.* 能接受新思想的
optimistic〔ˌɑptəˈmɪstɪk〕*adj.* 樂觀的
patient〔ˈpeʃənt〕*adj.* 有耐心的
practical〔ˈpræktɪkḷ〕*adj.* 現實的
professional〔prəˈfɛʃənḷ〕*adj.* 專業的
reliable〔rɪˈlaɪəbḷ〕*adj.* 可靠的
responsible〔rɪˈspɑnsəbḷ〕*adj.* 負責任的
sincere〔sɪnˈsɪr〕*adj.* 眞誠的
smart〔smɑrt〕*adj.* 聰明的
careful〔ˈkɛrfəl〕*adj.* 仔細的
steady〔ˈstɛdɪ〕*adj.* 沉著穩健的
strenuous〔ˈstrɛnjʊəs〕*adj.* 奮發的；努力的
tactful〔ˈtæktfəl〕*adj.* 機智的；圓滑的
thoughtful〔ˈθɔtfəl〕*adj.* 體貼的
wise〔waɪz〕*adj.* 有智慧的

3 政府輔導就業機構

服務站名	地址	電話	傳眞
板橋就業服務站	板橋市民族路 37 號	(02)29598856-7	(02)29587927
中壢就業服務站	中壢市長江路 87 號	(03)4259583-4	(03)4224420
新竹就業服務站	新竹市中華路 2 段 723 號	(03)5257041-2	(03)5265515
玉里就業服務站	玉里鎮光復路 160 號	(03)8882033	(03)8886140
竹北就業服務站	新竹縣竹北市福興路 576 號	(03)5542654-5	(03)5542567
花蓮就業服務站	花蓮就業國民三街 25 號	(03)8323262	(03)8356927
苗栗就業服務站	苗栗市中華路 143 號	(037)261017	(037)266341
豐原就業服務站	豐原市中山路 288 號	(04)5271812	(04)5253993
沙鹿就業服務站	台中縣沙鹿鎮中山路 493 號	(04)6624191	(04)6624282
彰化就業服務站	彰化市長壽街 202 號	(04)7239134	(04)7239858
南投就業服務站	南投市彰南路 2 段 117 號	(049)224094	(049)222834
岡山就業服務站	岡山鎮岡燕路 347 號	(07)6220253	(07)6224485
鳳山就業服務站	鳳山市中山東路 93 號	(07)7410243	(07)7410214
潮洲就業服務站	潮洲鎮昌明路 98 號	(08)7884358	(08)7883502
斗六就業服務站	斗六市中正路 16 巷 7 號	(05)5325105	(05)5345609
台東就業服務站	台東市新生路 230 號	(089)324042	(089)346854
北港就業服務站	北港鎮光明路 39 號	(05)7835644	(05)7820271
澎湖就業服務站	馬公市水源路 52 號	(06)9271207	(06)9261985
嘉義就業服務站	嘉義市北門街 92 號	(05)2783826	(05)2750841
新營就業服務站	新營市大同路 32 號	(06)6328700	(06)6321423
新店就業服務站	新店市北新路一段 80 號	(02)29179635	
新莊就業服務站	新莊市景德路 83 號	(02)29916380	

羅東就業服務站	羅東鎮公正路 209 之 2 號	(03)8882033	(03)3361134
中和就業服務站	中和市景平路 239 之 1 號	(02)29423237 (02)29423318	(02)29779906
三重就業服務站	三重市重新路 3 段 120 號	(02)29767157-8	(02)29779906
新竹工業區就業服務站	新竹市工業區中華路 22 號	(035)981940	
台中加工區就業服務站	台中縣潭子鄉台中加工出口區建國路 1 號	(04)5322113	
安平工業區就業服務站	台南市中華西街一段 67 號	(06)2648674	

4 政府就業服務網站一覽表

勞委會	http://www.cla.gov.tw/
勞委會職業訓練局	http://www.evta.gov.tw/
基隆區就業服務中心	http://job.evta.gov.tw/klesa/
台北區就業服務中心	http://job.evta.gov.tw/tpesa/
台中區就業服務中心	http://job.evta.gov.tw/tcesa/
台南區就業服務中心	http://job.evta.gov.tw/tnesa/
高雄區就業服務中心	http://job.evta.gov.tw/khesa/
台北市職業訓練中心	http://www.tvtc.gov.tw/
高雄市訓練就業中心	http://labor.kcg.gov.tw/taec/
青輔會	http://www.nyc.gov.tw/
退輔會	http://www.vac.gov.tw/dept3/
行政院原住民委員會	http://www.apc.gov.tw/
中華民國僑務委員會	http://www.ocac.gov.tw/
國軍人才招募中心	http://www.mnd.gov.tw/rdrc/
村里便民服務	http://village.gov.tw/
台北市就業服務中心—大台北才庫	http://www.esctcg.gov.tw/
台北縣就業服務網	http://www.goodjob.tpc.gov.tw/

5 私人就業服務網站一覽表

My Job 人力銀行	http://www.myjob.com.tw/
104 人力銀行	http://www.104.com.tw/
138 人力銀行	http://www.138.com.tw/
Career 就業情報網	http://www.career.com.tw/
168 人力銀行	http://www.168job.com.tw/
1001 就業中心	http://www.jobcenter.com.tw/
JobsDB.com 台灣，跨國就業網站	http://www.jobsdb.com.tw/tw/
88JOB 免費人力銀行	http://www.88job.com/
1111 人力銀行	http://www.1111.com.tw/
瑞強人力流通網	http://www.rejob.com.tw/
9999 泛亞人力銀行	http://www.9999.com.tw/
EEnet 電子新貴人力網	http://www.eenet.com.tw/newjob/main1.asp/

6 考選部九十四年度考試日期計劃表

考　試　名　稱	等　級	預定考試日期
公務人員初等考試	初　等	1月15日～1月16日
第一次專門職業及技術人員高等暨普通考試醫事人員、中醫師、心理師、呼吸治療師、營養師、獸醫人員考試	專技高考、普考	2月26日～2月27日
第一次專門職業及技術人員特種考試航海人員考試	相當專技高考、普考	3月26日開始
中醫師檢定考試		4月2日～4月4日
第一次專門職業及技術人員律師、會計師、建築師、技師、社會工作師、醫事人員、營養師、獸醫人員、中醫師、土地登記專業代理人檢覈筆試暨醫師、牙醫師檢覈筆試分階段考試		4月2日～4月4日
特種考試地方政府公務人員考試	三等、四等、五等	4月16日～4月18日
公務人員高等考試三級考試暨普通考試第一試	高考三級、普考	5月7日～5月8日
專門職業及技術人員普通考試導遊人員、領隊人員、記帳士考試	專技普考	5月21日～5月22日
專門職業及技術人員特種考試消防設備人員、不動產估價師、專責報關人員、保險從業人員考試	相當專技高考、普考、初等考試	5月28日～5月30日
專門職業及技術人員特種考試引水人、驗船師、漁船船員考試	相當專技高考、普考、初等考試	5月28日～5月30日
公務人員特種考試關務人員考試	三等、四等	6月4日～6月6日
公務人員特種考試稅務人員考試	三等、四等	6月4日～6月6日

考　試　名　稱	等　級	預定考試日期
第二次專門職業及技術人員特種考試航海人員考試	相當專技高考、普考	6月18日開始
公務人員高等考試三級考試暨普通考試第二試	高考三級普考	7月6日～7月10日
公務人員特種考試警察人員考試	三等、四等	7月16日～7月18日
第二次專門職業及技術人員高等暨普通考試醫事人員、中醫師、心理師、呼吸治療師、營養師、獸醫人員考試	專技高考、普考	7月23日～7月24日
公務人員特種考試民航人員考試	三等、四等	7月30日～8月1日
交通事業公路人員、鐵路人員升資考試	高員級、員級、佐級	8月6日～8月7日
第二次專門職業及技術人員律師、會計師、建築師、技師、社會工作師、醫事人員、營養師、獸醫人員、中醫師、土地登記專業代理人檢覈筆試暨醫師、牙醫師檢覈筆試分階段考試		8月13日～8月15日
第一次國軍上校以上軍官外職停役轉任公務人員檢覈筆試		8月13日～8月15日
專門職業及技術人員高等考試律師、會計師、社會工作師、民間之公證人、不動產估價師考試	專技高考	8月26日～8月28日
公務人員高等考試一級暨二級考試	高考一級、高考二級	9月3日～9月4日
公務人員特種考試外交領事人員考試	三　等	9月10日～9月12日
公務人員特種考試法務部調查局調查人員考試	三　等	9月10日～9月11日
第三次專門職業及技術人員特種考試航海人員考試	相當專技高考、普考	9月17日開始

考試名稱	等級	預定考試日期
專門職業及技術人員特種考試中醫師、心理師、呼吸治療師考試	相當專技高考	9月24日~9月25日
公務人員特種考試司法人員考試	三等、四等	10月8日~10月10日
公務人員升官等考試	簡任、薦任、委任	11月12日~11月14日
關務人員升官等考試	簡任、薦任	11月12日~11月14日
第二次國軍上校以上軍官外職停役轉任公務人員檢覈筆試		11月12日~11月14日
公務人員特種考試身心障礙人員考試	三等、四等、五等	11月25日~11月27日
第四次專門職業及技術人員特種考試航海人員考試	相當專技高考、普考	11月26日開始
專門職業及技術人員高等考試建築師、技師考試、普通考試不動產經紀人、地政士考試。	專技高考、普考	12月17日~12月19日

備註：一、九十四年國軍上校以上軍官轉任公務人員考試，如用人機關提報任用需求，將適時辦理公告。

二、九十四年公務人員特種考試社會福利工作人員考試，視考試規則研修進度及用人機關提報任用需求，適時辦理公告。

三、九十四年公務人員特種考試基層行政警察人員及基層消防警察人員考試，如用人機關提報任用需求，將適時辦理公告。

四、預定報名日期爲各該考試日期前二個半月左右，惟實際報名日期仍以考試公告之日期爲準。

五、表列考試及其考試日期必要時得予變更，並以考試公告爲準。

7 陸軍九十三年度志願役預備指揮軍官徵選辦法

1. **甄選人數：** 男性指揮軍官 200 人，女性指揮軍官 20 人。

2. **甄選對象：** 凡中華民國國籍具有學士學位之社會青年

3. **甄選資格：**

 ⑴ 學歷及年齡：具學士學位以上者。需年滿 20 至 27 歲（民國 66 年至 73 年底前出生者）。

 ⑵ 身高：男性 160 至 190 公分；女生 155 至 180 公分

 ⑶ 視力：兩眼視力 600 度以內，經矯正達 0.8 以上者，不計裸視。視差不得超過 400 度。

 ⑷ 顏面傷殘（如胎記、疤痕）、青蛙腿、扁平足、斷指等因素，經「指揮軍官」體檢醫院鑑定爲不合格者，不予報考。身體任何部分有刺青、紋身者，一律不合格。

 ⑸ 在校期間因品德言行方面有記大過以上處分，服役期間受記過以上或品德操守受申誡以上處分者，均不得報名。

4. **體檢時間：** 八月五日至九月二十一日

5. **報名日期：** 十月五至七日，早上八點至下午五點止，一律由考生親自報名。欲參加甄選者，需在報名前兩週的星期一上午八點起，至報名前一週的星期四晚上十二點止，先至國軍人才招募中心全球資訊網（www.mnd.gov.tw/rdrc），辦理「網路塡寫報名表」事宜。

6. **報名地點：**

 ⑴ 北部地區：

  ① 金六結營區 —— 宜蘭縣建軍路 45 號（宜蘭正聲電台旁）

  ② 國軍松山醫院 —— 台北市健康路 131 號

③ 國軍桃園總醫院 —— 桃園縣龍潭鄉中興路 168 號
④ 國軍新竹醫院 —— 新竹市武陵路 3 號

⑵ 中部地區：

① 中區招募中心 —— 台中市西屯區青海路二段 124 號
② 明德營區 —— 南投市民族路 512 號
③ 嘉義介壽營區 —— 嘉義市大雅路 2 段 206 號

⑶ 南部地區

① 網寮南營區 —— 台南永康市復興南路 235 號
② 國軍高雄總醫院 —— 高雄市中正一路 2 號
③ 國軍高雄總醫院屏東分院 —— 屏東市大湖路 58 巷 22 號

⑷ 花東地區

① 花蓮服務站 —— 花蓮市中山路 400 號
② 台東服務站 —— 台東市中興路 3 段 69 巷 100 號

⑸ 外島地區

① 金門服務站 —— 金門縣金湖鎮新市里自強路 21 號
② 澎湖服務站 —— 澎湖縣馬公市民生路 36 號
③ 馬港招待所 —— 連江縣南竿鄉馬祖村

7. **基本體能測驗**：十月二十二日（五）；早上七點半至下午六點

⑴ 測驗科目：

男性：① 一分鐘仰臥起坐 20 次以上。
② 一分鐘單槓引體向上，兩次以上。
③ 1600 公尺跑步，十分鐘以內

女性：① 一分鐘仰臥起坐 15 次以上。
② 屈臂懸計時 10 秒以上。
③ 1200 公尺跑步，八分鐘以內

8. **基本體能測驗地點：**

⑴ **北區**：國立陸軍高中（桃園縣中壢市中山東路四段 113 號）

⑵ **中區**：國立台中高工（台中市南區高工路 191 號）

⑶ **南區**：衛武營營區（高雄縣鳳山市自由路 451 號）

⑷ **東區**：南美崙營區（美崙山公園旁）

9. **智力測驗及筆試：**

⑴ **測驗日期**：十月二十三日（六）

⑵ **測驗地點**：

① **北區**：國立陸軍高中（桃園縣中壢市中山東路四段 113 號）

② **中區**：國立台中高工（台中市南區高工路 191 號）

③ **南區**：鳳甲高中（高雄縣鳳山市溜汽路 300 號）

④ **東區**：花蓮私立四維中學（花蓮市中山路一段 200 號）

10. **測驗時間及科目：**

8:00–8:20	8:20–9:10	9:30–10:20	10:40–11:30	13:00–13:50	14:10–16:00
指導說明	智力測驗	國　文	英　文	專業科目	口　試

11. **口試內容：** 以家庭狀況、學習過程、工作經驗、生涯規劃、軍事常識、時事新聞、一般常識等爲主。

12. **錄取標準：** 按總成績（國文＋英文＋專業科目＋證照、證書）排名決定錄取順序。具與報考官科相關之中華民國技術士證照甲級加十五分、乙級加十分，具全民英語能力分級檢定測驗中高級以上合格證書加五分。

13. **相關資訊：**

請參考國防部網站 www.mnd.gov.tw 相關網頁

國軍人才招募中心 0800-000050 http://www.mnd.gov.tw/rdrc

陸軍總部招募組 0800-096314 E-mail:rarmy@mnd.gov.tw

甄選官科及畢業系所專長對照表

<table>
<tr><th rowspan="2">甄選官科</th><th rowspan="2">大學系所</th><th colspan="2">測驗科目</th></tr>
<tr><th>共同科目</th><th>專業科目</th></tr>
<tr><td>步兵、砲兵、裝甲陸航、政戰</td><td>不限科系</td><td rowspan="9">國文、英文</td><td>無</td></tr>
<tr><td>化學（含女性）</td><td>化學、化工、物理、生物、核子工程學類</td><td>物理、化學</td></tr>
<tr><td>工兵（含女性）</td><td>建築、土木、水利工程學類</td><td>結構學</td></tr>
<tr><td>通信（含女性）</td><td>通信、電子、電機資訊工程及管理學類</td><td>電子學</td></tr>
<tr><td>運輸（含女性）</td><td>交通、運輸、機械車輛工程學類</td><td>運輸管理學</td></tr>
<tr><td>兵工（含女性）</td><td>機械、電機、電子車輛工程學類</td><td>電工機械</td></tr>
<tr><td>軍醫（含女性）</td><td>國內外醫學院校各系所</td><td>生物學概論</td></tr>
<tr><td>經理（含女性）</td><td>商、管理學類</td><td rowspan="2">管理學概論</td></tr>
<tr><td>行政（含女性）</td><td>不限科系</td></tr>
</table>

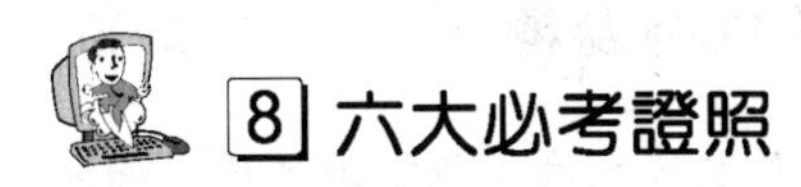

8 六大必考證照

1. ITE 資訊專業人員鑑定考試

目前已列入我國資訊業務委外招標加分項，詳細資料如下：

類　別	考試時間	適　用　產　業
系統分析	4、7、9、11 月	電腦軟體業
軟體設計	4、7、9、11 月	電腦軟體業、多媒體遊戲業
網路通訊	4、7、9、11 月	金融業、通訊業、消費服務業、多媒體遊戲業
資訊安全	4、7、9、11 月	金融業、通訊業、消費服務業、電腦軟體業
專案管理	7、11 月	電子業、製造業
嵌入式系統	9 月	電子業、通訊業
資料庫開發	7、11 月	金融業、電子業、通訊業、製造業、電腦軟體業
電子化學習	11 月	消費服務業、多媒體遊戲業
數位內容	9 月	多媒體遊戲業
數位內容報名費 3000 元整；其餘科目皆為 800 元整		
資料來源：www.itest.org.tw；www.csf.org.tw		

2. TQC 企業人才技能認證

在國內部分大專院校的推薦甄試，可獲得加分，詳細資料如下：

類　　別	認　　證　　項　　目	適　用　職　務
專業知識類	電子商務概論、初級會計	科技業、服務業
作業系統類	Windows98/Me/2000/XP	資訊業
辦公室軟體應用類	Word、Excel、PowerPoint 中英文輸入、數字輸入、中文聽打、電腦會計、網際網路應用	各行各業
資料庫應用類	Access、SQL Server	科技業、資訊業
程式設計類	VB 程式設計、VB 軟體開發	資訊業
工程製圖類	CAD2D、CAD3D、MDT、Pro/E	建築業、電子機械業
網頁設計類	FrontPage、HTML、ASP JavaScript	電子業、資訊業
影像處理類	PhotoImpact	資訊業
多媒體設計類	Flash	電子業、資訊業

3. 銀行業相關證照

測　驗　名　稱	測驗日期	報　名　期　間
第四屆理財規劃人員專業能力測驗	93/05/16	93/03/01～93/03/19
第五屆初階外匯人員專業能力測驗	93/06/20	93/03/22～93/04/09
第九期信託業業務人員信託業務專業測驗	93/08/15	93/05/31～93/06/18
第六屆初階授信人員專業能力測驗	93/09/19	93/06/21～93/07/09
第四屆進階授信人員專業能力測驗	93/09/19	93/06/21～93/07/09
第六期銀行內部控制基本測驗	93/10/17	93/07/12～93/07/30
第五屆理財規劃人員專業能力測驗	93/11/21	93/08/09～93/08/27
第十期信託業業務人員信託業務專業測驗	93/12/19	93/09/27～93/10/15
備註：相關資料查詢 www.tabf.org.tw		

4. 證券業相關證照

類　　別	測驗方式	測驗日期
證券商業務員證照	筆　試	93/09/05，93/12/05
證券商高級業務員證照	電腦應試	每週一至週五
證券投資分析人員證照 投信投顧業務員證照	筆　試	93/09/05，93/12/05
期貨商業務員證照	筆　試	93/09/05，93/12/05
證券交易分析人員	電腦應試	每週一至週五
票券商業務人員證照	電腦應試	每週一至週五
債券人員專業能力測驗	筆　試	十一月中旬
股務人員專業能力測驗	筆　試	十一月中旬
備註：相關資料查詢 www.sfi.org.tw/newsfi		

5. 保險業相關證照

類　　別	考試日期	相關資料查詢
人身保險業務員資格測驗合格證書	自10月2日起 每七日皆舉行一次測驗	www.lia-roc.org.tw 中華民國人壽保險商業同業公會
人身保險業務員中級專業課程測驗合格證書	9月5日、10月3日 11月7日、12月5日	www.lia-roc.org.tw 中華民國人壽保險商業同業公會
投資型保險商品業務員	10月17、31日，11月14、28日，12月19日	www.iiroc.org.tw 保險事業發展中心
風險管理師	11月20日	www.rmst.org.tw 中華民國風險管理學會

6. 英語認證

(1) TOEIC 多益測驗

考試日期	考場	報名日期
8月22日	台北、台中	6/28～7/23
9月19日	台北、桃園、高雄	7/26～8/20
10月17日	台北	8/23～9/17
11月21日	台北、台中、高雄	9/27～10/22
12月19日	台北、桃園	10/25～11/19
備註：相關參考資料 http://www.toeic.com.tw/		

成績	說明	成績	說明
10–300	初等級，僅能以簡單的語句應付基本需求	555–650	最高中等級，可應付工作上的基本對話
305–400	最高初等級，可以談論熟悉的話題	655–800	進階級，可應付工作上的對話需求，但若面臨緊急情況，仍可能出錯
405–550	中等級，可應付日常會話	805–990	最高進階級，可有效參與大多數談話
備註：台灣平均總分為 538 分			

(2) TOEFL 托福考試

週一至週五及每月第三個週六。

上午場 8:00～13:00；下午場 13:00～18:00；週六 12:00～17:00

（註：測驗中心將視報考人數多寡決定開放的測驗日期、場次）

托福筆試與電腦測驗分數對照表											
筆試	677	650	620	600	570	550	530	500	473	450	400
電腦	300	280	260	250	230	213	197	173	150	133	97

(3) GEPT 全民英檢

級別	類別	測驗日期	報名日期	備註
初級	初試	94/1/8 94/6/25	93/10/28～11/3 94/4/14～20	相當於國中程度
	複試	94/4/2～3 94/9/10～11	94/2/17～25 94/7/29～8/10	
中級	初試	94/2/19 94/8/6	93/12/9～15 94/6/2～8	相當於高中程度
	複試	94/4/30～5/1 94/10/15～16	94/3/9～18 94/8/23～9/2	
中高級	初試	94/5/21 94/10/29	94/3/24～30 94/9/1～7	相當於大學非英語系程度
	複試	94/7/16 94/12/24	94/6/7～17 94/11/15～25	
高級	初試	94/9/24	94/8/11～17	相當於大學英語系所程度
	複試	94/12/10～11	94/10/21～11/2	
優級	尚未公佈 94 年考試相關資訊			相當於受過高等教育之母語人士
詢問報考事項：02-2369-7127；語言訓練中心網址：www.gept.org.tw				

9 進修頻道▸就業潛力無限的研究所

業別	高潛力學系	學校
軟體業	資工、電子電機所	台大、清大、交大 中央、台科大、元智 中原
IC 設計業	電子電機所	台大、清大、交大、成大 中央、中正、台科大
TFT-LCD 業	電子、光電、化學 化工應化、材料所	台大、交大、清大、成大 中央、中山、台科大 中原、淡江、元智
半導體業	電子、電機、材料機械 工業工程、資訊工程 電物、電信所	台大、清大、交大、成大 中山、中央、長庚
網路通訊業	電子、電信、電機 資工所	台大、清大、交大、成大 元智
會計業	會計系	台大、政大、東吳
法律業	法律所、科法所	台大、政大、東吳、中興 中正、交大
企業法務 （法務、商標、專利）	法律所、科法所	台大、政大、東吳、交大
金融業	保險、統計、數學 財務金融、財務工程 資訊、資管	台大、政大、中山

10 職訓局在職進修訓練課程

在失業率高漲，裁員風盛行的世代裡，如何把金飯碗拿穩，已成了人人關心的話題，下表列出由政府補助的職訓課程：

課程名稱	上課地點	費用	相關資訊
不動產仲介實務班（10/16-11/6）	彰化縣	自費 1770 補助 1770	地址：彰化市卦山路 5 號 電話：04-7222609 訓練單位：彰化縣總工會
電腦輔助製圖班（10/18-11/24）	台南市	自費 5120 補助 5120	地址：台南市中區大埔街 50 號 電話：06-2154389 訓練單位：台南市總工會
客家美食班（11/1-11/30）	苗栗縣	自費 8680 補助 8680	地址： 苗栗縣通霄鎮中山路 28 號 電話：037-758308 訓練單位：苗栗縣外燴服務工作人員職業工會
中餐烹調進修（10/18-10/25）	苗栗縣	自費 5170 補助 5170	地址：嘉義市和平路 63 號 2 樓 e-mail：chef.cvc1688@msa.hinet.net 訓練單位：中華民國餐飲業工會全國聯合會
網路行銷建置 B 班（10/16-10/24）	高雄市	自費 1700 補助 1700	地址：高雄市前鎮區 e-mail：chien.yen@msa.hinet.net 訓練單位：高雄市機械業產業工會聯合會
機械業網路維護技術班 B 班（11/3-11/12）	高雄市	自費 2000 補助 2000	地址：高雄市前鎮區 e-mail：chien.yen@msa.hinet.net 訓練單位：高雄市機械業產業工會聯合會

課程名稱	上課地點	費用	相關資訊
數位影像攝影進階班（10/23-10/31）	台北市	自費 3200 補助 3200	地址：台北市大同區延平北路 3 段 24 號 電話：02-2597-0321 訓練單位：中華民國照相錄影研究發展協會
不動產人員基礎訓練 B 班（11/6-11/14）	花蓮縣	自費 1840 補助 1840	地址：花蓮市中山路 654 之 1 號 電話：03-8562843 訓練單位：花蓮縣不動產服務職業工會
網頁設計應用班（10/25-11/15）	苗栗縣	自費 2840 補助 2840	地址：苗栗市 e-mail：miaolitu@ms52.hinet.net 訓練單位：苗栗縣產業總工會
平面顯示器產業技術人才訓練 C 班（11/2-11/30）	台北市	自費 3600 補助 3600	地址：台北市內湖區民權東路 6 段 109 號 6 樓 e-mail：Daphneyu@teema.org.tw 訓練單位：台灣區電機電子工業同業公會
AUTO CAD 工業電腦繪圖 B 班（10/13-11/26）	新竹市	自費 5700 補助 5700	地址：新竹縣竹北市縣政八街 25 號 1 樓 e-mail：His12345@ms19.hinet.net 訓練單位：新竹縣工業會
旅行社經營管理實務訓練 D 班領團人員進階班（11/1-12/1）	台南市	自費 2450 補助 2450	地址：台南市中區東門路 1 段 358 號 5 樓之 2 電話：06-2358476 訓練單位：台南市旅行商業同業公會
不動產經紀營業員專業訓練班 C 班（10/27-11/10）	雲林縣	自費 3270 補助 3270	地址：雲林縣斗六市雲林路 2 段 142 號 電話：05-5336540 訓練單位：雲林縣不動產仲介經紀商業同業公會
邏輯電路（10/25-12/22）	台北縣	自費 2296 補助 2236	地址：248 台北縣五股工業區五權路 17 號 7 樓 電話：02-89903608#115 訓練單位：行政院勞委會職業訓練局北區職業訓練中心

課程名稱	上課地點	費用	相關資訊
文書排版與視窗操作（11/1-12/31）	台北縣	自費 1688 補助 1102	地址：248 台北縣五股工業區五權路17號7樓 電話：02-89903608#115 訓練單位：行政院勞委會職業訓練局北區職業訓練中心
網路架設（11/8-12/22）	高雄市	自費 2680 補助 3747	地址：高雄市前鎮區凱旋四路 105 號 電話：07-8210171#309 訓練單位：行政院勞委會職業訓練局南區職業訓練中心
CNC 車床班（11/1-12/27）	高雄市	自費 2304 補助 2304	地址：高雄市前鎮區凱旋四路 105 號 電話：：07-8210171#303 訓練單位：行政院勞委會職業訓練局南區職業訓練中心
影像處理（11/1-12/3）	高雄市	自費 1950 補助 2750	地址：高雄市前鎮區凱旋四路 105 號 電話：：07-8210171#303 訓練單位：行政院勞委會職業訓練局南區職業訓練中心
電腦輔助機械設計繪圖（11/1-12/31）	桃園縣	自費 1614 補助 2014	地址：桃園縣楊梅鎮秀才路 851 號 電話：03-4855368 訓練單位：行政院勞委會職業訓練局桃園職業訓練中心
電腦綜合控制（11/1-12/31）	桃園縣	自費 1803 補助 2203	地址：桃園縣楊梅鎮秀才路 851 號 電話：03-4855368 訓練單位：行政院勞委會職業訓練局桃園職業訓練中心
冷凍空調實務班（11/1-12/31）	桃園縣	自費 1556 補助 1956	地址：桃園縣楊梅鎮秀才路 851 號 電話：03-4855368 訓練單位：行政院勞委會職業訓練局桃園職業訓練中心

課程名稱	上課地點	費用	相關資訊
可程式控制實務班（11/1-12/31）	桃園縣	自費 1902 補助 2302	地址：桃園縣楊梅鎮秀才路 851 號 電話：03-4855368 訓練單位：行政院勞委會職業訓練局桃園職業訓練中心
單晶片控制系統班（11/1-12/31）	桃園縣	自費 1768 補助 2168	地址：桃園縣楊梅鎮秀才路 851 號 電話：03-4855368 訓練單位：行政院勞委會職業訓練局桃園職業訓練中心
服裝班（11/1-12/31）	桃園縣	自費 1468 補助 1868	地址：桃園縣楊梅鎮秀才路 851 號 電話：03-4855368 訓練單位：行政院勞委會職業訓練局桃園職業訓練中心珍
廣告設計電腦繪圖班(11/1-12/31)	桃園縣	自費 1814 補助 2214	地址：桃園縣楊梅鎮秀才路 851 號 電話：03-4855368 訓練單位：行政院勞委會職業訓練局桃園職業訓練中心
電腦美工與影像處理實務班（10/13-11/15）	台南市	自費 4200 補助 4200	地址：台南市中區西門路 2 段 48 號 電話：06-2200699 訓練單位：德鍵企業有限公司附設職業訓練中心
網際網路資料庫程式設計班（10/13-11/15）	台南市	自費 5210 補助 5210	地址：台南市中區西門路 2 段 48 號 電話：06-2200699 訓練單位：德鍵企業有限公司附設職業訓練中心

課程名稱	上課地點	費用	相關資訊
ASP.Net 網頁設計工程師訓練班（11/1-11/19）	嘉義市	自費 3180 補助 3180	地址：嘉義市吳鳳南路 94 號 電話：05-2224171#5023 訓練單位：中國石油公司訓練所
多媒體網頁設計基礎班 front page(B)（10/18-11/18）	高雄市	自費 2390 補助 2390	地址：高雄市小港區中鋼路 3 號 電話：07-8010111#2842 訓練單位：中國造船股份有限公司
PhotoImpact 影像處理系統班（10/25-10/29）	台南市	自費 1460 補助 1460	地址：台灣糖業股份有限公司訓練中心 電話：06-2696771 訓練單位：台南市東區生產路 56 號
採購暨工程發包作業電子化研究班（11/22-11/26）	台南市	自費 1330 補助 1330	地址：台灣糖業股份有限公司訓練中心 電話：06-2696771 訓練單位：台南市東區生產路 56 號
ACCESS 資料庫進階班（11/1-11/5）	台南市	自費 1460 補助 1460	地址：台灣糖業股份有限公司訓練中心 電話：06-2696771 訓練單位：台南市東區生產路 56 號
平地造林訓練班（11/9-11/12）	台南市	自費 1570 補助 1570	地址：台灣糖業股份有限公司訓練中心 電話：06-2696771 訓練單位：台南市東區生產路 56 號
Linux 系統基礎訓練班（11/8-11/12）	台南市	自費 1460 補助 1460	地址：台灣糖業股份有限公司訓練中心 電話：06-2696771 訓練單位：台南市東區生產路 56 號
廣域與區域網路基礎訓練班（11/15-11/19）	台南市	自費 1460 補助 1460	地址：台灣糖業股份有限公司訓練中心 電話：06-2696771 訓練單位：台南市東區生產路 56 號

※ 政府補助職業訓練課程眾多，詳情請上網查詢，

網址：http://training.evta.gov.tw/

11. 應徵職務英譯表

Account Executive —— 業務經理
Accountant —— 會計；會計師
Accounting Assistant —— 會計助理
Accounting Clerk —— 記帳員
Accounting Manager —— 會計部經理
Accounting Secretary —— 會計書記

* * *

Accounting Staff —— 會計人員
Accounting Supervisor —— 會計主管
Adjunct Professor —— 兼任教授
Administrator —— 管理者；行政官
Administration Manager —— 行政經理
Administration Staff —— 行政人員

* * *

Administrative Assistant —— 行政助理
Administrative Clerk —— 行政辦事員
Administrative Coordinator —— 行政協調人員
Administrative Staff —— 行政人員
Advertising Staff —— 廣告工作人員
Adviser —— 指導教授
Airlines Sales Representative —— 航空公司機票訂位人員

Airlines Staff —— 航空公司職員
Analyst —— 分析師
Application Engineer —— 應用工程師
Architect —— 建築師
Assayer —— 化驗師
Assistant —— 助教
Assistant Dean —— 副院長

* * *

Assistant Engineer —— 助理工程師
Assistant Manager —— 副理
Assistant Production Manager —— 副廠長
Associate Professor —— 副教授
Aurist —— 耳科醫師
Bank Officer —— 銀行辦事員
Bond Analyst —— 證券分析師

* * *

Bond Dealer —— 證券交易人
Bond Trader —— 證券交易人
Bookkeeper —— 簿記員
Business Controller —— 業務主任
Business Manager —— 業務經理
Buyer —— 採購人員
Cardmember Service Representative — 卡友服務代表
Cashier —— 出納員

Certified Public Account ———— 檢定合格會計師

Chemical Engineer ———— 化學工程師

Chemist ———— 藥劑師；藥商

Chief Accountant ———— 會計主任

Chief Engineer ———— 總工程師

Chief Nurse ———— 護理長

Civil Engineer ———— 土木工程師

* * *

Clerk ———— 文書；辦事員；店員；職員

Clerk Typist ———— 文書打字

Clerk Typist & Secretary ———— 文書打字兼秘書

Comptroller ———— 主計；會計主任

Computer Data Input Operator ———— 電腦資料輸入員

Computer Engineer ———— 電腦工程師

Computer Processing Operator ———— 電腦處理操作員

* * *

Computer System Manager ———— 電腦系統經理

Computer Training Staff ———— 電腦訓練人員

Computer Translator ———— 電腦翻譯員

Consulting Engineer ———— 顧問工程師

Controller ———— 主計員；組長、處長

Coordinator ———— 協調人員

Copy Editor ———— 整理原稿的編輯

Copy Reader ———— 校訂人；原稿之訂正與編輯者

Copywriter —— 廣告文字撰稿人員
Counselor —— 法律顧問；律師
Credit Analyst —— 信用調查員
Customer Service Personnel —— 客服人員
Data Processing Clerk —— 資料處理人員
Dealer —— 商人；業者
Dean —— 院長

*　　　*　　　*

Dean of General Affairs —— 總務長
Dean of Students —— 訓導長
Dean of Studies —— 教務長
Dentist —— 牙醫師
Dermatologist —— 皮膚科醫師
Distribution Coordinator —— 產銷協調者
Do-all —— 事務員

*　　　*　　　*

Doctor —— 醫師
Door Keeper —— 守衛
EDP Auditor —— 電子資料處理稽核員
EDP Manager —— 電子資料處理經理
Economic Research Assistant —— 經濟研究助理
Editor —— 編輯；主筆
Editorial Assistant —— 助理編輯
Electrical Engineer —— 電機工程師

Electronics Staff —— 電子人員
Engineer —— 機械師；技師；工程師
Engineering Technician —— 工程技師
English Instructor —— 英語教師
Executive Director —— 常務董事
Export Clerk —— 出口部人員
Export Sales Manager —— 外銷部經理

*　　*　　*

Export Sales Staff —— 外銷部職員
Export Secretary —— 外銷部秘書
Executive Interpreter —— 執行翻譯
Executive Secretary —— 執行秘書
Filing Clerk —— 檔案管理員
Finance Executive —— 財政計劃釐定人
Financial Controller —— 財務主任

*　　*　　*

Financial Reporter —— 財務報告人
Flight Attendant —— 空服員
Foreman —— 領班；工頭
FX(Foreign Exchange) Clerk —— 外匯職員
FX Settlement Clerk —— 外匯清算人員
Free-lance Translator —— 自由翻譯者
Free-lance Writer —— 自由作家
Full-time Professor —— 專任教授

Fund Manager ———— 財務經理

General Administration ———— 總行政

General Auditor ———— 審計長

General Manager ———— 總經理

Ground Hostess ———— 女性地勤人員

Guest Professor ———— 客座教授

Hardware Engineer ———— 硬體工程師

* * *

Herb Doctor ———— 中醫師

Import Coordinator ———— 進口協調人員

Import Liaison Staff ———— 進口聯絡人員

Instructor ———— 講師

Instructor of Military Training ———— 教官

Insurance Actuary ———— 保險公司的理賠員

Insurance Broker ———— 保險經紀人員

* * *

Interior Staff ———— 內政人員

Internal Auditor ———— 國內查帳員

International Grain Trader ———— 國際穀物貿易商

International Sales Staff ———— 國際行銷人員

Intern Doctor ———— 實習醫師

Interpreter ———— 口譯員

Janitor ———— 工友

Judicial Doctor —— 法醫
Junior Engineer —— 工程員
Junior Manager —— 襄理
Laryngologist —— 婦科醫師
Law Office Secretary —— 法務秘書
Lawyer —— 律師
Lecturer —— 講師

* * *

Legal Advisor —— 法律顧問
Librarian —— 圖書館員
Line Supervisor —— 生產線管理師
Maintenance Engineer —— 維修工程師
Management Consultant —— 管理顧問
Management Coordinator —— 管理協調者
Manager —— 經理

* * *

Manufacturing Engineer —— 製造工程師
Manufacturing Worker —— 生產員工
Market Analyst —— 市場分析師
Market Development Manager —— 市場開發經理
Marketing Executive —— 市務主任
Marketing Manager —— 市務經理
Marketing Officer —— 市務主任
Marketing Assistant —— 行銷助理

Marketing Executive ———— 行銷主管
Marketing Officer ———— 銷售人員
Marketing Personnel ———— 銷售人員
Marketing Planner ———— 行銷企劃人員
Marketing Representative ———— 銷售代表
Marketing Research Manager ———— 市場研究經理
Mechanical Engineer ———— 機械工程師

*　　*　　*

Medical Officer ———— 軍醫
Mining Engineer ———— 採礦工程師
Mechanic ———— 技工
Money Market Dealer ———— 金融業者
Music Teacher ———— 音樂老師
Naval Architect ———— 造船工程師
Nurse ———— 護士

*　　*　　*

Obstetrician ———— 產科醫師
Oculist ———— 眼科醫師
Office Accountant ———— 會計
Office Assistant / Manager ———— 助理/經理
Office Boy ———— 小弟
Office Clerk ———— 職員；辦事員
Office Staff ———— 職員
Office Worker ———— 職員

Operational Manager —— 管理經理
Operations Clerk —— 操作員
Package Designer —— 包裝設計員
Part-time Professor —— 兼任教授
Passenger Reservation Staff —— 預訂乘客票位的職員
Pediatrician —— 小兒科醫師
Personnel Clerk —— 人事部職員

* * *

Personnel Staff —— 人事部職員
Pharmacist —— 藥劑師
Physician —— 内科醫師
Placement Coordinator —— 配置協調員
Planner —— 設計者；策劃人員
Plant Manager —— 廠長
Plastic Surgeon —— 整型醫師

* * *

Postal Clerk —— 郵政人員
Practice Nurse —— 實習護士
President —— 總裁
Private Secretary —— 私人秘書
Product Manager —— 生產部經理
Production Control Specialist —— 生產管制專家
Production Engineer —— 製造工程師
Production Manager —— 廠長

Professional Staff —— 專業人員
Professor —— 教授
Programmer —— 電腦程式設計人員
Project Staff —— 策劃人員
Promotional Manager —— 推廣部經理
Proofreader —— 校對員
Psychiatrist —— 精神科醫師

* * *

Purchasing Agent —— 採購經紀人(進貨員)
Quality Control Engineer —— 品管工程師
Real Estate Registration Agent —— 土地代書
Real Estate Staff —— 不動產人員
Receptionist —— 接待員
Recruitment Coordinator —— 招募協調人員
Regional Manager —— 區域經理

* * *

Remittance Clerk —— 匯款人員
Representative —— 代表
Reporter —— 記者;通訊員
R & D Engineer —— 研發工程師
Research Assistant —— 研究助理
Research Trainee —— 研究見習生
Researcher —— 研究人員
Resident Doctor —— 住院醫師

Restaurant Manager —— 餐廳經理
Rewrite Person —— 做報紙改寫工作的編輯或記者
Sales Administration Clerk —— 銷售行政人員
Sales and Planning Staff —— 銷售計畫員
Sales Assistant —— 銷售助理
Sales Clerk —— 店員；售貨員
Sales Coordinator —— 銷售協調者

* * *

Sales Engineer —— 銷售技師
Sales Executive —— 行銷主管
Sales Liaison Staffer —— 銷售連絡人
Salesman —— 推銷員
Sales Manager —— 業務經理
Salesperson —— 業務員；店員
Sales Promotion Manager —— 業務推廣部經理

* * *

Sales Representative —— 業務代表
Sales Supervisor —— 業務管理者
School Registrar —— 學校註冊主任
Secretarial Assistant —— 秘書助理
Secretarial Clerk —— 秘書
Secretary —— 秘書
Secretary / Office Clerk —— 秘書/辦事員
Securities Custody Clerk —— 保安人員

Security Officer —— 安全人員
Senior Accountant —— 高級會計員
Senior Consultant —— 高級顧問
Senior Engineer —— 高級工程師
Senior Secretary —— 高級秘書
Surveying Engineer —— 測量工程師
Service Manager —— 服務部經理

* * *

Settlement Clerk —— 清算人員
Shipping Clerk —— 負責貨物打包及裝運的人員
Shop Coordinator —— 商店經理
Simultaneous Interpreter —— 同步翻譯員
Skilled Worker —— 技術工人
Software Engineer —— 軟體工程師
Staff Assistant —— 助理

* * *

Staff Engineer —— 工程師
Stock Broker —— 股票經紀人
Sub-Manager —— 襄理
Supervisor —— 監工；管理人
Surgeon —— 外科醫師
Surveyor —— 測量員
Systems Adviser —— 系統顧問
Systems Engineer —— 系統工程師

Systems Operator —— 系統操作員

Technical Editor —— 具技術知識的編輯

Technical Liaison —— 技術連絡

Technical Liaison Manager —— 技術連絡經理

Technical Management —— 技術管理

Technical Translator —— 具技術知識的翻譯員

Technical Worker —— 技術工人

* * *

Technician —— 技術員

Tour Guide —— 觀光導遊

Trade Finance Executive —— 進出口財務主管

Trainee Manager —— 管理受訓人員的經理

Translation Checker —— 翻譯核對員

Translator —— 翻譯員

Trust Banking Executive —— 銀行高級職員

* * *

Typing / Shipping Clerk —— 打字/送貨員

Typist —— 打字員

Veterinarian —— 獸醫師

Vice President —— 副總裁

Visiting Professor —— 客座教授

Wordprocessor Operator —— 文字處理操作員

12 全國大專院校名稱英譯表

英文校名	中文校名
National Taiwan University	國立台灣大學
National Taiwan Normal University	國立師範大學
National Chengchi University	國立政治大學
National Taipei University	國立台北大學
National Tsing Hua University	國立清華大學
National Chiao Tung University	國立交通大學
National Cheng Kung University	國立成功大學
National Central University	國立中央大學
National Sun Yat-sen University	國立中山大學
National Chung Cheng University	國立中正大學
National Chung Hsing University	國立中興大學
Chinese Culture University	中國文化大學
Chung Shan Medical University	中山醫學大學
Central Police University	中央警察大學
China Medical University	中國醫藥大學
National Dong Hwa University	國立東華大學
National Kaohsiung Normal University	國立高雄師範大學
Taipei Medical University	台北醫學大學
Kaohsiung Medical University	高雄醫學大學
National Yang-Ming University	國立陽明大學

英文校名	中文校名
National Changhua University of Education	國立彰化師範大學
The National Open University	國立空中大學
National Chiayi University	國立嘉義大學
National University of Kaohsiung	國立高雄大學
National Chi Nan University	國立暨南國際大學
National Taiwan Ocean University	國立台灣海洋大學
National Taiwan University of Arts	國立台灣藝術大學
Taipei National University of The Arts	國立台北藝術大學
National Hualien Teachers College	國立花蓮師範學院
National Ping-Tung Teachers College	國立屏東師範學院
National Hsin Chu Teachers College	國立新竹師範學院
National Taichung Teachers College	國立台中師範學院
Taipei Municipal Teachers College	台北市立師範學院
National Taipei Teachers College	國立台北師範學院
National Taitung Teachers College	國立台東師範學院
National Tainan Teachers College	國立台南師範學院
Chung Cheng Institute of Technology	中正理工學院
Fu Hsing Kang College	政治作戰學校

英　文　校　名	中　文　校　名
Chinese Military Academy	陸軍軍官學校
Chinese Naval Academy	海軍軍官學校
Chinese Air Force Academy	空軍官校
National Defense Medical Center	國防醫學院
National Defense Management College	國防管理學院
National College of Physical Education and Sports	國立體育學院
National Taiwan College of Physical Education	國立台灣體育學院
Taipei Physical Education College	台北市立體育學院
Fu Jen Catholic University	天主教輔仁大學
Soochow University	東吳大學
Tatung University	大同大學
Da-Yeh University	大葉大學
Chung Yuan Christian University	中原大學
Chung Hua University	中華大學
Yuan Ze University	元智大學
Shin Hsin University	世新大學
Tunhai University	東海大學
Chang Gung University	長庚大學
Chang Jung Christian University	長榮大學
Nanhua University	南華大學

英文校名	中文校名
I-Shou University	義守大學
Aletheia University	眞理大學
Tamkang University	淡江大學
Feng Chia University	逢甲大學
Huafan University	華梵大學
Tzu Chi University	慈濟大學
Shih Chien University	實踐大學
Ming Chuan University	銘傳大學
Providence University	靜宜大學
National Pingtung University of Science & Technology	國立屏東科技大學
National Yunlin University of Science & Technology	國立雲林科技大學
National Taipei University of Technology	國立台北科技大學
National Taiwan University of Science and Technology	國立台灣科技大學
National Kaohsiung First University of Science and Technology	國立高雄第一科技大學
Southern Taiwan University of Technology	南台科技大學
Kun Shan University of Technology	崑山科技大學
Shu-Te University	樹德科技大學

英文校名	中文校名
Hungkuang University	弘光科技大學
Chaoyang University of Technology	朝陽科技大學
Chia Nan University of Pharmacy & Science	嘉南藥理科技大學
Lunghwa University of Science and Technology	龍華科技大學
Cheng Shiu Institute of Technology	正修科技大學
National Kaohsiung University of Applied Sciences	國立高雄應用科技大學
Ching Yun University	清雲科技大學
Leader University	立德管理學院
Kainan University	開南管理學院
Toko University	稻江科技暨管理學院
Fo Guang University	佛光人文社會學院
Hsuan Chuang University	玄奘人文社會學院
Tainan National College Of The Arts	台南藝術學院
Tajen Institute of Technology	大仁技術學院
Ta Hwa Institute of Technology	大華技術學院
Ling Tung College	嶺東技術學院
Chungtai Institute of Health Sciences and Technology	中台醫護技術學院
Chungchou Institute of Technology	中州技術學院

英　文　校　名	中　文　校　名
Chung Kuo Institute of Technology	中國技術學院
China Institute of Technology	中華技術學院
Yuanpei University of Science and Technology	元培科學技術學院
National Taichung Institute of Technology	國立台中技術學院
National Taipei College of Business	國立台北商業技術學院
Yung Ta Institute of Technology & Commerce	永達技術學院
Kuang Wu Institute of Technology	光武技術學院
Oriental Institute of Technology	亞東技術學院
National Ilan Institute of Technology	國立宜蘭技術學院
Takming College	德明技術學院
Tung Nan Institute of Technology	東南技術學院
Tainan Woman's College of Arts & Technology	台南女子技術學院
National Huwei Institute of Technology	國立虎尾技術學院
Chang Gung Institute of Technology	長庚技術學院
Nanya Institute of Technology	南亞技術學院
De-Lin Institute of Technology	德霖技術學院
Chien Kuo Institute of Technology	建國技術學院

英　文　校　名	中　文　校　名
National Pingtung Institute of Commerce	國立屏東商業技術學院
National Kaohsiung Institute of Marine Technology	國立高雄海洋技術學院
Jin Wen Institute of Technology	景文技術學院
National Chin-Yi Institute of Technology	國立勤益技術學院
St. John's & St. Mary's Institute of Technology	新埔技術學院
Air Force Institute of Technology	空軍航空技術學校
Taiwan Police College	台灣警察專科學校
Chung Hwa College of Medical Technology	中華醫事學院
China College of Marine Technology and Commerce	中國海事商業專校
National Tainan Institute of Nursing	國立台南護理專校
Cardinal Tien College of Nursing	耕莘護理專校
National Taichung Nursing College	國立台中護理專校
Chung Yu Junior College of Business Administration	崇右企業管理專科學校
Kang-Ning Junior College of Medical Care and Management	康寧醫護暨管理專科學校
Hwa Hsia College of Technology and Commerce	華夏工商專科學校

13 大專院校科系名稱英譯表

英　文　系　名	中　文　系　名
Department of Foreign Languages and Literatures	外文系
Department of Chinese Literature	中文系
Department of History	歷史系
Department of Philosophy	哲學系
Department of Anthropology	人類學系
Department of Library and Information Science	圖書資訊系
Department of Japanese Literature and Language	日文系
Department of Drama and Theatre	戲劇系
Department of Mathematics	數學系
Department of Physics	物理系
Department of Chemistry	化學系
Department of Geosciences	地質學系
Department of Zoology	動物學系
Department of Botany	植物學系
Department of Psychology	心理學系
Department of Geography	地理系
Department of Atmospheric Sciences	大氣科學系
Department of Political Science	政治系

英　文　系　名	中　文　系　名
Department of Economics	經 濟 系
Department of Sociology	社 會 系
Department of Social Work	社 工 系
Department of Medicine	醫 學 系
Department of Dentistry	牙 醫 系
Department of Pharmacy	藥 學 系
Department of Oriental Languages and Literature	東方語文學系
Department of Western Languages and Literature	西方語文學系
Department of English	英 語 系
Department of Education	教 育 系
Department of Journalism	新 聞 系
Department of Mass Communication	大衆傳播系
Department of Diplomacy	外 交 系
Department of International Relations	國際關係系
Department of Law Science	法 律 系
Department of Public Administration	公共行政學系
Department of Risk Management and Insurance	風險管理與保險系
Department of Land Administration	地 政 系
Department of International Trade	國 貿 系
Department of Banking	銀行系；金融系
Department of Accounting	會 計 系
Department of Statistics	統 計 系

英 文 系 名	中 文 系 名
Department of Business Administration	企 管 系
Department of Finance	財務金融學系
Department of Public Finance	財 政 系
Department of Industrial Management	工業管理系
Department of Tourist Industry	觀光事業系
Department of Korean Language and Literature	韓 語 系
Department of German	德 語 系
Department of Russian Language and Literature	俄 語 系
Department of Arabic Language and Literature	阿拉伯語文學系
Department of French	法 語 系
Department of Spanish	西班牙語文學系
Department of Arts	藝 術 系
Department of Music	音 樂 系
Department of Dance	舞 蹈 系
Department of Architectural Engineering	建築工程系
Department of Chemical Engineering	化 工 系
Department of Civil Engineering	土木工程系
Department of Electrical Engineering	電機工程系
Department of Industrial Engineering	工業工程系
Department of Mechanical Engineering	機械工程系

英文系名	中文系名
Department of Engineering and System Science	工程與系統科學系
Department of Nuclear Science	原子科學系
Department of Aeronautical Engineering	航空工程系
Department of Aeronautics and Astronautics	航空太空工程學系
Department of Communication Engineering	電信工程系
Department of Electronic Engineering	電子工程系
Department of Information Management	資訊管理學系
Department of Computer Science and Information Engineering	資訊工程學系
Department of Engineering Science	工程科學系
Department Industrial Design	工業設計系
Department of Environmental Engineering	環境工程系
Department of Textile Engineering	紡織工程學系
Department of Biology	生 物 系
Department of Life Science	生命科學系
Department of Biochemical Science and Technology	生化科技系
Department of Geology	地質學系
Department of Electrophysics	電子物理學系
Department of Surveying Engineering	測量及空間資訊學系

英 文 系 名	中 文 系 名
Department of Transportation and Logistics Management	交通與物流管理學系
Department of Water & Soil Maintenance Engineering	水土保持系
Department of Earth Sciences	地球科學系
Department of Management Science	管理科學系
Department of Hydraulic Engineering	水利工程學系
Department of Pathology	病理學系
Department of Medical Technology	醫事技術學系
Department of Medical Engineering	醫學工程系
Department of Public Health	公共衛生學系
Department of Veterinary Medicine	獸 醫 系
School of Nursing	護理學系
Department of Physical Therapy	物理治療學系
School of Occupational Therapy	職能治療學系
Department of Agricultural Extension	農業推廣學系
Department of Agricultural Economics	農業經濟學系
Department of Agricultural Chemistry	農業化學系
Department of Agronomy	農藝學系
Department of Food Science	食品科學系
Department of Food & Nutrition	食品營養系
Department of Forestry	森 林 系
Department of Horticulture	園 藝 系

英　文　系　名	中　文　系　名
Department of Entomology	昆 蟲 系
Department of Animal Science	畜產學系
Department of Plant Pathology and Microbiology	植物病理與微生物學系
Department of Home Economics	家 政 系
Department of Physical Education	體 育 系
Department of Aquatic Biosciences	水產生物系
Department of Oceanography	海洋學系
Department of Transportation Management	航運管理系
Department of Navigation	航海學系
Department of River & Harbor Engineering	河海工程學系
Department of Mechanical and Marine Engineering	機械與輪機工程學系
Department of System Engineering and Naval Architecture	系統工程暨造船學系

14 國語羅馬拼音對照表

注音	拼音	注音	拼音	注音	拼音	注音	拼音	注音	拼音	注音	拼音
ㄅ		**ㄇ**		ㄉㄜ	te	ㄊㄨㄥ	tung	ㄌㄥ	leng	ㄍㄨㄟ	kuei
ㄅㄚ	pa	ㄇㄚ	ma	ㄉㄟ	tei	**ㄋ**		ㄌㄧ	li	ㄍㄨㄣ	kun
ㄅㄞ	pai	ㄇㄞ	mai	ㄉㄥ	teng	ㄋㄚ	na	ㄌㄧㄚ	lia	ㄍㄨㄥ	kung
ㄅㄢ	pan	ㄇㄢ	man	ㄉㄧ	ti	ㄋㄞ	nai	ㄌㄧㄤ	liang	ㄍㄨㄛ	kuo
ㄅㄤ	pang	ㄇㄤ	mang	ㄉㄧㄠ	tiao	ㄋㄢ	nan	ㄌㄧㄠ	liao	**ㄎ**	
ㄅㄠ	pao	ㄇㄠ	mao	ㄉㄧㄝ	tieh	ㄋㄤ	nang	ㄌㄧㄝ	lieh	ㄎㄚ	ka
ㄅㄟ	pei	ㄇㄟ	mei	ㄉㄧㄢ	tien	ㄋㄠ	nao	ㄌㄧㄢ	lien	ㄎㄞ	kai
ㄅㄣ	pen	ㄇㄣ	men	ㄉㄧㄥ	ting	ㄋㄜ	ne	ㄌㄧㄣ	lin	ㄎㄢ	kan
ㄅㄥ	peng	ㄇㄥ	meng	ㄉㄧㄡ	tiu	ㄋㄟ	nei	ㄌㄧㄥ	ling	ㄎㄤ	kang
ㄅㄧ	pi	ㄇㄧ	mi	ㄉㄨㄛ	to	ㄋㄣ	nen	ㄌㄧㄡ	liu	ㄎㄠ	kao
ㄅㄧㄠ	piao	ㄇㄧㄠ	miao	ㄉㄡ	tou	ㄋㄥ	neng	ㄌㄨㄛ	lo	ㄎㄜ	ke
ㄅㄧㄝ	pieh	ㄇㄧㄝ	mieh	ㄉㄨ	tu	ㄋㄧ	ni	ㄌㄡ	lou	ㄎㄣ	ken
ㄅㄧㄢ	pien	ㄇㄧㄢ	mien	ㄉㄨㄢ	tuan	ㄋㄧㄤ	niang	ㄌㄨ	lu	ㄎㄥ	keng
ㄅㄧㄣ	pin	ㄇㄧㄣ	min	ㄉㄨㄟ	tui	ㄋㄧㄠ	niao	ㄌㄨㄢ	luan	ㄎㄡ	kou
ㄅㄧㄥ	ping	ㄇㄧㄥ	ming	ㄉㄨㄣ	tun	ㄋㄧㄝ	nieh	ㄌㄨㄣ	lun	ㄎㄨ	ku
ㄅㄛ	po	ㄇㄧㄡ	miu	ㄉㄨㄥ	tung	ㄋㄧㄢ	nien	ㄌㄨㄥ	lung	ㄎㄨㄚ	kua
ㄅㄨ	pu	ㄇㄛ	mo	**ㄊ**		ㄋㄧㄣ	nin	ㄌㄩ	lu	ㄎㄨㄞ	kuai
ㄆ		ㄇㄡ	mou	ㄊㄚ	ta	ㄋㄧㄥ	ning	ㄌㄩㄢ	luan	ㄎㄨㄢ	kuan
ㄆㄚ	pa	ㄇㄨ	mu	ㄊㄞ	tai	ㄋㄧㄡ	niu	ㄌㄩㄝ	lueh	ㄎㄨㄤ	kuang
ㄆㄞ	pai	**ㄈ**		ㄊㄢ	tan	ㄋㄨㄛ	no	**ㄍ**		ㄎㄨㄟ	kuei
ㄆㄢ	pan	ㄈㄚ	fa	ㄊㄤ	tang	ㄋㄡ	nou	ㄍㄚ	ka	ㄎㄨㄣ	kun
ㄆㄤ	pang	ㄈㄢ	fan	ㄊㄠ	tao	ㄋㄨ	nu	ㄍㄞ	kai	ㄎㄨㄥ	kung
ㄆㄠ	pao	ㄈㄤ	fang	ㄊㄜ	te	ㄋㄨㄢ	nuan	ㄍㄢ	kan	ㄎㄨㄛ	kuo
ㄆㄟ	pei	ㄈㄟ	fei	ㄊㄥ	teng	ㄋㄨㄣ	nun	ㄍㄤ	kang	**ㄏ**	
ㄆㄣ	pen	ㄈㄣ	fen	ㄊㄧ	ti	ㄋㄨㄥ	nung	ㄍㄠ	kao	ㄏㄚ	ha
ㄆㄥ	peng	ㄈㄥ	feng	ㄊㄧㄠ	tiao	ㄋㄩ	nu	ㄍㄜ	ke	ㄏㄞ	hai
ㄆㄧ	pi	ㄈㄛ	fo	ㄊㄧㄝ	ten	ㄋㄩㄝ	nueh	ㄍㄟ	kei	ㄏㄢ	han
ㄆㄧㄠ	piao	ㄈㄡ	fou	ㄊㄧㄢ	tien	**ㄌ**		ㄍㄣ	ken	ㄏㄤ	hang
ㄆㄧㄝ	pieh	ㄈㄨ	fu	ㄊㄧㄥ	ting	ㄌㄚ	la	ㄍㄥ	keng	ㄏㄠ	hao
ㄆㄧㄢ	pien	**ㄉ**		ㄊㄨㄛ	to	ㄌㄞ	lai	ㄍㄡ	kou	ㄏㄟ	hei
ㄆㄧㄣ	pin	ㄉㄚ	ta	ㄊㄡ	tou	ㄌㄢ	lan	ㄍㄨ	ku	ㄏㄣ	hen
ㄆㄧㄥ	ping	ㄉㄞ	tai	ㄊㄨ	tu	ㄌㄤ	lang	ㄍㄨㄚ	kua	ㄏㄥ	heng
ㄆㄛ	po	ㄉㄢ	tan	ㄊㄨㄢ	tuan	ㄌㄠ	lao	ㄍㄨㄞ	kuai	ㄏㄜ	ho
ㄆㄡ	pou	ㄉㄤ	tang	ㄊㄨㄟ	tui	ㄌㄜ	le	ㄍㄨㄢ	kuan	ㄏㄡ	hou
ㄆㄨ	pu	ㄉㄠ	tao	ㄊㄨㄣ	tun	ㄌㄟ	lei	ㄍㄨㄤ	kuang	ㄏㄨ	hu

注音	羅馬拼音
ㄏㄨㄚ	hua
ㄏㄨㄞ	huai
ㄏㄨㄢ	huan
ㄏㄨㄤ	huang
ㄏㄨㄟ	hui
ㄏㄨㄣ	hun
ㄏㄨㄥ	hung
ㄏㄨㄛ	huo
ㄐ	
ㄐㄧ	chi
ㄐㄧㄚ	chia
ㄐㄧㄤ	chiang
ㄐㄧㄠ	chiao
ㄐㄧㄝ	chieh
ㄐㄧㄣ	chin
ㄐㄧㄥ	ching
ㄐㄧㄡ	chiu
ㄐㄩㄥ	chiung
ㄐㄩ	chu
ㄐㄩㄝ	chueh
ㄐㄩㄣ	chun
ㄑ	
ㄑㄧ	chi
ㄑㄧㄚ	chia
ㄑㄧㄤ	chiang
ㄑㄧㄠ	chiao
ㄑㄧㄝ	chieh
ㄑㄧㄢ	chien
ㄑㄧㄣ	chin
ㄑㄧㄥ	ching
ㄑㄧㄡ	chiu
ㄑㄩㄥ	chiung
ㄑㄩ	chu
ㄑㄩㄢ	chuan
ㄑㄩㄝ	chueh
ㄑㄩㄣ	chun
ㄒ	
ㄒㄧ	hsi
ㄒㄧㄚ	hsia
ㄒㄧㄤ	hsiang
ㄒㄧㄠ	hsiao
ㄒㄧㄝ	hsieh
ㄒㄧㄢ	hsien
ㄒㄧㄣ	hsin
ㄒㄧㄥ	hsing
ㄒㄧㄡ	hsiu
ㄒㄩㄥ	hsiung
ㄒㄩ	hsu
ㄒㄩㄢ	hsuan
ㄒㄩㄝ	hsueh
ㄒㄩㄣ	hsun
ㄓ	
ㄓㄚ	cha
ㄓㄞ	chai
ㄓㄢ	chan
ㄓㄤ	chang
ㄓㄠ	chao
ㄓㄜ	che
ㄓㄟ	chei
ㄓㄣ	chen
ㄓㄥ	cheng
ㄓㄨㄛ	cho
ㄓㄡ	chou
ㄓㄨ	chu
ㄓㄨㄚ	chua
ㄓㄨㄞ	chuai
ㄓㄨㄢ	chuan
ㄓㄨㄤ	chuang
ㄓㄨㄟ	chui
ㄓㄨㄣ	chun
ㄓㄨㄥ	chung
ㄔ	
ㄔㄚ	cha
ㄔㄞ	chai
ㄔㄢ	chan
ㄔㄤ	chang
ㄔㄠ	chao
ㄔㄜ	che
ㄔㄣ	chen
ㄔㄥ	cheng
ㄔㄨㄛ	cho
ㄔㄡ	chou
ㄔㄨ	chu
ㄔㄨㄚ	chua
ㄔㄨㄞ	chuai
ㄔㄨㄢ	chuan
ㄔㄨㄤ	chuang
ㄔㄨㄟ	chui
ㄔㄨㄣ	chun
ㄔㄨㄥ	chung
ㄔ	chih
ㄕ	
ㄕㄚ	sha
ㄕㄞ	shai
ㄕㄢ	shan
ㄕㄤ	shang
ㄕㄠ	shao
ㄕㄜ	she
ㄕㄟ	shei
ㄕㄣ	shen
ㄕㄥ	sheng
ㄕ	shih
ㄕㄡ	shou
ㄕㄨ	shu
ㄕㄨㄚ	shua
ㄕㄨㄞ	shuai
ㄕㄨㄢ	shuan
ㄕㄨㄤ	shuang
ㄕㄨㄟ	shui
ㄕㄨㄣ	shun
ㄕㄨㄛ	shuo
ㄖ	
ㄖㄢ	jan
ㄖㄤ	jang
ㄖㄠ	jao
ㄖㄜ	je
ㄖㄣ	jen
ㄖㄥ	jeng
ㄖ	jih
ㄖㄨㄛ	jo
ㄖㄡ	jou
ㄖㄨ	ju
ㄖㄨㄢ	juan
ㄖㄨㄟ	jui
ㄖㄨㄣ	jun
ㄖㄨㄥ	jung
ㄗ	
ㄗㄚ	tsa
ㄗㄞ	tsai
ㄗㄢ	tsan
ㄗㄤ	tsang
ㄗㄠ	tsao
ㄗㄜ	tse
ㄗㄟ	tsei
ㄗㄣ	tsen
ㄗㄥ	tseng
ㄗㄨㄛ	tso
ㄗㄡ	tsou
ㄗㄨ	tsu
ㄗㄨㄢ	tsuan
ㄗㄨㄟ	tsui
ㄗㄨㄣ	tsun
ㄗㄨㄥ	tsung
ㄗ	tzu
ㄘ	
ㄧㄠ	yao
ㄧㄝ	yeh
ㄘㄚ	tsa
ㄘㄞ	tsai
ㄘㄢ	tsan
ㄘㄤ	tsang
ㄘㄠ	tsao
ㄘㄜ	tse
ㄘㄣ	tsen
ㄘㄥ	tseng
ㄘㄨㄛ	tso
ㄘㄡ	tsou
ㄘㄨ	tsu
ㄘㄨㄢ	tsuan
ㄘㄨㄟ	tsui
ㄘㄨㄣ	tsun
ㄘㄨㄥ	tsung
ㄘ	tzu
ㄙ	
ㄙㄚ	sa
ㄙㄞ	sai
ㄙㄢ	san
ㄙㄤ	sang
ㄙㄠ	sao
ㄙㄜ	se
ㄙㄣ	sen
ㄙㄥ	seng
ㄙㄨㄛ	so
ㄙㄡ	sou
ㄙㄨ	su
ㄙㄨㄢ	suan
ㄙㄨㄟ	sui
ㄙㄨㄣ	sun
ㄙㄨㄥ	sung
ㄙ	szu
ㄧ	
ㄧㄚ	ya
ㄧㄞ	yai
ㄧㄤ	yang
ㄧㄠ	yao
ㄧㄝ	yeh
ㄧㄢ	yen
ㄧ	yi
ㄧㄣ	yin
ㄧㄥ	ying
ㄧㄡ	yu
ㄨ	
ㄨㄚ	wa
ㄨㄞ	wai
ㄨㄢ	wan
ㄨㄤ	wang
ㄨㄟ	wei
ㄨㄣ	wen
ㄨㄥ	weng
ㄨㄛ	wo
ㄨ	wu
ㄩ	
ㄩㄥ	yung
ㄩ	yu
ㄩㄢ	yuan
ㄩㄝ	yueh
ㄩㄣ	yun
ㄚ	a
ㄞ	ai
ㄢ	an
ㄤ	ang
ㄠ	ao
ㄜ	e
ㄣ	en
ㄥ	eng
ㄡ	ou
ㄦ	erh

15 台灣縣市名稱英譯表

Taipei City	台北市	Yunlin Hsien	雲林縣
Kaohsiung City	高雄市	Chiayi Hsien	嘉義縣
Taichung City	台中市	Tainan Hsien	台南縣
Tainan City	台南市	Kaohsiung Hsien	高雄縣
Keelung City	基隆市	Pingtung Hsien	屏東縣
Hsinchu City	新竹市	Yilan Hsien	宜蘭縣
Chiayi City	嘉義市	Hualian Hsien	花蓮縣
Taipei Hsien	台北縣	Taitung Hsien	台東縣
Taoyuan Hsien	桃園縣	Nantou Hsien	南投縣
Hsinchu Hsien	新竹縣	Penghu Hsien	澎湖縣
Miaoli Hsien	苗栗縣	Makung	馬　公
Taichung Hsien	台中縣	Kinmen (Quemoy)	金　門
Changhwa Hsien	彰化縣	Matsu	馬　祖

全國最完整的文法書☆☆☆

文法寶典

劉 毅 編著

這是一套想學好英文的人必備的工具書，作者積多年豐富的教學經驗，針對大家所不了解和最容易犯錯的地方，編寫成一套完整的文法書。

本書編排方式與衆不同，首先給讀者整體的概念，再詳述文法中的細節部分，內容十分完整。文法說明以圖表爲中心，一目了然，並且務求深入淺出。無論您在考試中或其他書中所遇到的任何不了解的問題，或是您感到最煩惱的文法問題，查閱**文法寶典**均可迎刃而解。例如：哪些副詞可修飾名詞或代名詞？(P.228)；什麼是介副詞？(P.543)；那些名詞可以當副詞用？(P.100)；倒裝句(P.629)、省略句(P.644)等特殊構句，爲什麼倒裝？爲什麼省略？原來的句子是什麼樣子？在**文法寶典**裏都有詳盡的說明。

例如，有人學了**觀念錯誤的**「假設法現在式」的公式，

If＋現在式動詞⋯⋯，主詞＋shall (will, may, can)＋原形動詞

只會造：If it rains, I will stay at home.

而不敢造：If you ***are*** right, I ***am*** wrong.

If I ***said*** that, I ***was*** mistaken.

(If 子句不一定用在假設法，也可表示條件子句的直說法。)

可見如果學文法不求徹底了解，反而成爲學習英文的絆腳石，對於這些易出錯的地方，我們都特別加以說明(詳見 P.356)。

文法寶典每册均附有練習，只要讀完本書、做完練習，您必定信心十足，大幅提高對英文的興趣與實力。

◉ 全套五册，售價*900*元。市面不售，請直接向本公司購買。

●學習出版公司門市部●

台北地區：台北市許昌街 10 號 2 樓 TEL:(02)2331-4060·2331-9209
台中地區：台中市綠川東街 32 號 8 樓 23 室
TEL:(04)2223-2838

求職英語

修　　編／王淑平
發 行 所／學習出版有限公司　☎ (02) 2704-5525
郵撥帳號／0512727-2 學習出版社帳戶
登 記 證／局版台業 *2179* 號
印 刷 所／裕強彩色印刷有限公司
台北門市／台北市許昌街 10 號 2 F　☎ (02) 2331-4060·2331-9209
台中門市／台中市綠川東街 32 號 8 F 23 室　☎ (04) 2223-2838
台灣總經銷／紅螞蟻圖書有限公司　☎ (02) 2795-3656
美國總經銷／Evergreen Book Store　☎ (818) 2813622
本公司網址　www.learnbook.com.tw
電子郵件　learnbook@learnbook.com.tw

售價：新台幣二百八十元正

2004 年 12 月 1 日二版二刷

ISBN 957-519-729-1